NOT EXACTLY YOUR
ORDINARY FAIRY TALE

Sure, there's a kingdom—but all the men including the King are away.

Sure, there's a beautiful princess—but she doesn't seem able to do much with her looks.

Sure, there's an evil Queen (well, not exactly a Queen, but at least a countess)—but she keeps on stealing the show.

And then, of course, there's the Prince.

One thing you can say about him. Prince Charming he definitely is not . . .

Once On A Time

A fairy tale that's aimed over the heads of kids—to split every grown-up's sides.

Once on a Time

A. A. Milne

A SIGNET BOOK

NEW AMERICAN LIBRARY

SIGNET, SIGNET CLASSIC, MENTOR, ONYX, PLUME, MERIDIAN
and NAL BOOKS are published by NAL PENGUIN INC.,
1633 Broadway, New York, New York 10019

First Signet Printing, August, 1988

1 2 3 4 5 6 7 8 9

PRINTED IN THE UNITED STATES OF AMERICA

1

The King of Euralia Has a Visitor to Breakfast

KING MERRIWIG OF Euralia sat at breakfast on his castle walls. He lifted the gold cover from the gold dish in front of him, selected a trout, and conveyed it carefully to his gold plate. He was a man of simple tastes, but when you have an aunt with the newly acquired gift of turning anything she touches into gold, you must let her practice sometimes. In another age it might have been fretwork.

"Ah," said the King, "here you are, my dear." He searched for his napkin, but the Princess had already kissed him lightly on the top of the head, and was sitting in her place opposite him.

"Good morning, Father," she said; "I'm a little late, aren't I? I've been riding in the forest."

"Any adventures?" asked the King casually.

"Nothing, except it's a beautiful morning."

"Ah, well, perhaps the country isn't what it

was. Now when I was a young man, you simply couldn't go into the forest without an adventure of some sort. The extraordinary things one encountered! Witches, giants, dwarfs . . . It was there that I first met your mother," he added thoughtfully.

"I wish I remembered my mother," said Hyacinth.

The King coughed and looked at her a little nervously.

"Seventeen years ago she died, Hyacinth, when you were only six months old. I have been wondering lately whether I haven't been a little remiss in leaving you motherless so long."

The Princess looked puzzled. "But it wasn't your fault, dear, that Mother died."

"Oh, no, no, I'm not saying that. As you know, a dragon carried her off and—well, there it was. But supposing"—he looked at her shyly —"I had married again."

The Princess was startled.

"Who?" she asked.

The King peered into his flagon. "Well," he said, "there *are* people."

"If it had been somebody *very* nice," said the Princess wistfully, "it might have been rather lovely."

The King gazed earnestly at the outside of his flagon.

"Why 'might have been'?" he said.

The Princess was still puzzled. "But I'm grown up," she said; "I don't want a mother so much now."

The King turned his flagon around and studied the other side of it.

"A mother's—er—tender hand," he said, "is—er—never—" and then the outrageous thing happened.

It was all because of a birthday present to the King of Barodia, and the present was nothing less than a pair of seven-league boots. The King being a busy man, it was a week or more before he had an opportunity of trying those boots. Meanwhile he used to talk about them at meals, and he would polish them up every night before he went to bed. When the great day came for the first trial of them to be made, he took a patronizing farewell of his wife and family, ignored the many eager noses pressed against the upper windows of the Palace, and sailed off. The motion, as perhaps you know, is a little disquieting at first, but one soon gets used to it. After that it is fascinating. He had gone some two thousand miles before he realized that there might be difficulty about finding his way back. The difficulty proved at least as great as he had anticipated. For the rest of that day he toured backward and forward across the country; and it was by the merest accident that a very angry

King shot in through an open pantry window in the early hours of the morning. He removed his boots and went softly to bed. . . .

It was, of course, a lesson to him. He decided that in the future he must proceed by a recognized route, sailing lightly from landmark to landmark. Such a route his Geographers prepared for him—an early-morning constitutional, of three hundred miles or so, to be taken ten times before breakfast. He gave himself a week in which to recover his nerve and then started out on the first of them.

Now the Kingdom of Euralia adjoined that of Barodia, but whereas Barodia was a flat country, Euralia was a land of hills. It was natural then that the Court Geographers, in search of landmarks, should have looked toward Euralia; and over Euralia accordingly, about the time when cottage and castle alike were breakfasting, the King of Barodia soared and dipped and soared and dipped again.

"A mother's—er—tender hand," said the King of Euralia, "is—er—never—good gracious! What's that?"

There was a sudden rush of air; something came for a moment between his Majesty and the sun; and then all was quiet again.

"What was it?" asked Hyacinth, slightly alarmed.

"Most extraordinary," said the King. "It left in my mind an impression of ginger whiskers and large boots. Do we know anybody like that?"

"The King of Barodia," said Hyacinth, "has red whiskers, but I don't know about his boots."

"But what could he have been doing up there? Unless—"

There was another rush of wind in the opposite direction; once more the sun was obscured, and this time, plain for a moment for all to see, appeared the rapidly dwindling back view of the King of Barodia on his way home to breakfast.

Merriwig rose with dignity.

"You're quite right, Hyacinth," he said sternly; "it *was* the King of Barodia."

Hyacinth looked troubled.

"He oughtn't to come over anybody's breakfast table quite so quickly as that. Ought he, Father?"

"A lamentable display of manners, my dear. I shall withdraw now and compose a stiff note to him. The amenities must be observed."

Looking as severe as a naturally jovial face would permit him, and wondering a little if he had pronounced *amenities* right, he strode to the library.

The library was his Majesty's favourite apartment. Here in the mornings he would discuss affairs of state with his Chancellor, or receive any distinguished visitors who were come to his kingdom in search of adventure. Here in the afternoon, with a copy of *What to Say to a Wizard* or some such book taken at random from the shelves, he would give himself up to meditation.

And it was the distinguished visitors of the morning who gave him most to think about in the afternoon. There were at this moment no fewer than seven different Princes engaged upon seven different enterprises, to whom, in the event of a successful conclusion, he had promised the hand of Hyacinth and half his kingdom. No wonder he felt that she needed the guiding hand of a mother.

The stiff note to Barodia was not destined to be written. He was still hesitating between two different kinds of nib when the door was flung open and the fateful name of the Countess Belvane was announced.

The Countess Belvane! What can I say which will bring home to you that wonderful, terrible, fascinating woman? Mastered as she was by an overweening ambition, utterly unscrupulous in her methods of achieving her purpose, none the less her adorable humanity betrayed itself in a passion for diary-keeping and a devotion to the simpler forms of lyrical verse. That she is the villain of the piece, I know well; in his *Euralia Past and Present* the eminent historian Roger Scurvilegs does not spare her; but that she had her great qualities, I should be the last to deny.

She had been writing poetry that morning, and she wore green. She always wore green when the Muse was upon her: a pleasing habit which, whether as a warning or an inspiration, modern poets might do well to imitate. She carried an enormous diary under her arm, and, in her mind, several alternative ways of putting down her reflections on her way to the Palace.

"Good morning, dear Countess," said the King, rising only too gladly from his nibs; "an early visit."

"You don't mind, your Majesty?" said the Countess anxiously. "There was a point in our conversation yesterday about which I was not quite certain—"

"What *were* we talking about yesterday?"

"Oh, your Majesty," said the Countess, "affairs of state," and she gave him that wicked, innocent, impudent, and entirely scandalous look which he never could resist, and you couldn't either, for that matter.

"Affairs of state, of course." The King smiled.

"Why, I made a special note of it in my diary."

She laid down the enormous volume and turned lightly over the pages.

"Here we are! *'Thursday*. His Majesty did me the honour to consult me about the future of his daughter, the Princess Hyacinth. Remained to tea and was very . . .' I can't quite make this word out."

"Let *me* look," said the King, his rubicund face becoming yet more rubicund. "It looks like 'charming,' " he said casually.

"Fancy!" said Belvane. "Fancy my writing that! I put down just what comes into my head at the time, you know." She made a gesture with her hand indicative of someone who puts down just what comes into her head at the time, and returned to her diary. " 'Remained to tea, and was very charming. Mused afterwards on the mutability of life!' " She looked up at him with wide-open eyes. "I often muse when I'm alone," she said.

The King still hovered over the diary.

"Have you any more entries like—like that last one? May I look?"

"Oh, your Majesty! I'm afraid it's *quite* private." She closed the book quickly.

"I thought I saw some poetry," said the King.

"Just a little ode to a favourite linnet. It wouldn't interest your Majesty."

"I adore poetry," said the King, who had himself written a rhymed couplet which could be said either forward or backward, and in the latter position was useful for removing enchantments. According to the eminent historian Roger Scurvilegs, it had some vogue in Euralia and went like this:

"Bo, boll, bill, bole.
Wo, woll, will, wole."

A pleasing idea, temperately expressed.

The Countess, of course, was only pretending. Really she was longing to read it. "It's quite a little thing," she said.

" 'Hail to thee, blithe linnet,
Bird thou clearly art,
That from bush or in it
Pourest thy full heart!
And leads the feathered choir in song
Taking the treble part.' "

"Beautiful," said the King, and one must agree with him. Many years after, another poet called Shelley plagiarized the idea, but handled it in a more artificial, and, to my way of thinking, decidedly inferior manner.

"Was it a real bird?" said the King.

"An old favourite."

"Was it pleased about it?"

"Alas, your Majesty, it died without hearing it."

"Poor bird!" said his Majesty; "I think it would have liked it."

Meanwhile Hyacinth, innocent of the nearness of a mother, remained on the castle walls and tried to get on with her breakfast. But she

13

made little progress with it. After all, it *is* annoying continually to look up from your bacon, or whatever it is, and see a foreign monarch passing overhead. Eighteen more times the King of Barodia took Hyacinth in his stride. At the end of the performance, feeling rather giddy, she went down to her father.

She found him alone in the library, a foolish smile upon his face, but no sign of a letter to Barodia in front of him.

"Have you sent the Note yet?" she asked.

"Note? Note?" he said, bewildered, "what —oh, you mean the Stiff Note to the King of Barodia? I'm just planning it, my love. The exact shade of stiffness, combined with courtesy, is a little difficult to hit."

"I shouldn't be too courteous," said Hyacinth; "he came over eighteen more times after you'd gone."

"Eighteen, eighteen, eight—my dear, it's outrageous."

"I've never had such a crowded breakfast before."

"It's positively insulting, Hyacinth. This is no occasion for Notes. We will talk to him in a language that he will understand."

And he went out to speak to the Captain of his Archers.

2

The Chancellor of Bardoia Has a Long Walk Home

ONCE MORE IT was early morning on the castle walls.

The King sat at his breakfast table, a company of archers drawn up in front of him.

"Now you all understand," he said. "When the King of Baro—when a certain—well, when I say 'when,' I want you all to fire your arrows into the air. You are to take no aim; you are just to shoot your arrows upward, and—er—I want to see who gets highest. Should anything—er—should anything brush up against them on their way—not of course that it's liikely—well, in that case—er—in that case, something will—er—brush up against them. After all, what *should*?"

"Quite so, Sire," said the Captain, "or rather, not at all."

"Very well. To your places."

Each archer fitted an arrow to his bow and

took up his position. A lookout man had been posted. Everything was ready.

The King was decidedly nervous. He wandered from one archer to another, asking after this man's wife and family, praising the polish on that man's quiver, or advising him to stand with his back a little more to the sun. Now and then he would hurry off to the lookout man on a distant turret, point out Barodia on the horizon to him, and hurry back again.

The lookout knew all about it.

"Royalty over," he bellowed suddenly.

"When!" roared the King, and a cloud of arrows shot into air.

"Well done!" cried Hyacinth, clapping her hands. "I mean, how could you? You might have hurt him."

"Hyacinth," said the King, turning suddenly; "you here?"

"I have just come up. Did you hit him?"

"Hit who?"

"The King of Barodia, of course."

"The King of . . . My dear child, what could the King of Barodia be doing here? My archers were aiming at a hawk that they saw in the distance." He beckoned to the Captain. "Did you hit that hawk?" he asked.

"With one shot only, Sire. In the whisk—in the tail feathers."

The King turned to Hyacinth.

"With one shot only in the whisk—in the tail feathers," he said. "What was it, my dear, that you were saying about the King of Barodia?"

"Oh, Father, you are bad. You hit the poor man right in the whisker."

"His Majesty of Barodia! And in the whisker! My dear child, this is terrible! But what can he have been doing up there? Dear, dear, this is really most unfortunate. I must compose a note of apology about this."

"I should leave the first note to him," said Hyacinth.

"Yes, yes, you're right. No doubt he will wish to explain how he came to be there. Just a moment, dear."

He went over to his archers, who were drawn up in line again.

"You may take your men down now," he said to the Captain.

"Yes, your Majesty."

His Majesty looked quickly round the castle walls, and then leant confidentially toward the Captain.

"Er—which was the man who—er"—he fingered his cheek—"er—quite so. The one on the left? Ah, yes." He went to the man on the left and put a bag of gold into his hand.

"You have a very good style with the bow, my man. Your wrist action is excellent. I have never seen an arrow go so high."

The company saluted and withdrew. The King and Hyacinth sat down to breakfast.

"A little mullet, my dear?" he said.

The Hereditary Grand Chancellor of Barodia never forgot that morning, nor did he allow his wife to forget it. His opening, "That reminds me, dear, of the day when . . ." though the signal of departure for any guests, allowed no escape for his family. They had to have it.

And, indeed, it was a busy day for him. Summoned to the Palace at nine o'clock, he found the King nursing a bent whisker and in the very vilest of tempers. His Majesty was for war at once; the Chancellor leaned toward the Stiff Note.

"At least, your Majesty," he begged, "let me consult the precedents first."

"There is no precedent," said the King coldly, "for such an outrage as this."

"Not precisely, Sire; but similar unfortunate occurrences have—occurred."

"It was worse than an occurrence."

"I should have said an outrage, your Majesty. Your late lamented grandfather was unfortunate enough to come beneath the spell of the King of Araby, under which he was compelled—or perhaps I should say preferred—to go about on his hands and knees for several weeks. Your Majesty may recall how the people in their great loyalty adopted a similar mode of progression. Now although your Majesty's case is not precisely on all fours—"

"Not at all on all fours," said the King coldly.

"An unfortunate metaphor; I should say that although your Majesty's case is not parallel, the procedure adopted in your revered grandfather's case—"

"I don't care what *you* do with your whiskers; I don't care what *anybody* does with his whiskers," said the King, still soothing his own tenderly; "I want the King of Euralia's blood." He looked round the Court. "To anyone who will bring me the head of the King, I will give the hand of my daughter in marriage."

There was a profound silence. . . .

"Which daughter?" said a cautious voice at last.

"The eldest," said the King.

There was another profound silence. . . .

"My suggestion, your Majesty," said the Chancellor, "is that for the present there should be merely an exchange of Stiff Notes; and that meanwhile we scour the kingdom for an enchanter who shall take some pleasant revenge for us upon his Majesty of Euralia. For instance, Sire, a king whose head has been permanently fixed on upside-down lacks somewhat of that regal dignity which alone can command the respect of his subjects. A couple of noses, again, placed at different angles, so they cannot both be blown together—"

"Yes, yes," said the King impatiently, "*I'll* think of the things, if once you can find the enchanter. But they are not so common nowadays. Besides, enchanters are delicate things to work with. They have a habit of forgetting which side they are on."

The Chancellor's mouth drooped piteously.

"Well," said the King condescendingly, "I'll tell you what we'll do. You may send *one* Stiff Note and then we will declare war."

"Thank you, your Majesty," said the Chancellor.

So the Stiff Note was dispatched. It pointed out that his Majesty of Barodia, while in the act of taking his early-morning constitutional, had been severely insulted by an arrow. This arrow, though fortunately avoiding the more vital parts of his Majesty's person, went so far as to wound a favourite whisker. For this the fullest reparation must be made . . . and so forth and so on.

Euralia's reply was not delayed. It expressed the deepest concern at the unhappy accident which had overtaken a friendly monarch. On the morning in question, his Majesty had been testing his archers in a shooting competition at a distant hawk; which competition, it might interest his Majesty of Barodia to know, had been won by Henry Smallnose, a bowman of considerable promise. In the course of the competition it was noticed that a foreign body of some sort brushed up against one of the arrows, but as this in no way affected the final placing of the competitors, little attention was paid to it. His Majesty of Barodia might rest assured that the King had no wish to pursue the matter further. Indeed, he was always glad to welcome his Barodian Majesty on these occasions. Other shooting competitions would be arranged from time to time, and if his Majesty happened to be passing at the moment, the King of Euralia hoped that he would come down and join them. Trusting that her Majesty and their Royal Highnesses were well . . . and so on and so forth.

The Grand Chancellor of Barodia read this answer to his Stiff Note with a growing feeling of uneasiness. It was he who had exposed his Majesty to this fresh insult; and, unless he could soften it in some way, his morning at the Palace might be a painful one.

As he entered the precincts, he wondered whether the King would be wearing the famous boots, and whether they kicked seven leagues as easily as they strode them. He felt more and more that there were notes which you could break gently, and notes which you couldn't. . . .

Five minutes later, as he started on his twenty-one mile walk home, he realized that this was one of the ones which you couldn't.

*   *   *

This, then, was the real reason of the war between Euralia and Barodia. I am aware that in saying this I differ from the eminent historian Roger Scurvilegs. In Chapter IX of his immortal work, *Euralia Past and Present*, he attributes the quarrel between the two countries to quite other causes. The King of Barodia, he says, demanded the hand of the Princess Hyacinth for his eldest son. The King of Euralia made some commonplace condition as that his Royal Highness should first ride his horse up a glassy mountain in the district, a condition which his Majesty of Barodia strongly resented. I am afraid that Roger is incurably romatic; I have had to speak to him about it before. There was nothing of the sentimental in the whole business, and the facts are exactly as I have narrated them.

3

The King of Euralia Draws His Sword

NO DOUBT YOU have already guessed that it was the Countess Belvane who dictated the King of Euralia's answer. Left to himself, Merriwig would have said, "Serve you jolly well right for stalking over my kingdom." His repartee was never very subtle. Hyacinth would have said, "Of course we're *awfully* sorry, but a whisker isn't *very* bad, is it? and you really *oughtn't* to come to breakfast without being asked." The Chancellor would have scratched his head for a long time, and then said, "Referring to Chap. VII, Para. 259 of the *King's Regulations*, we notice . . ."

But Belvane had her own way of doing things; and if you suggest that she wanted to make Barodia's declaration of war inevitable, well, the story will show whether you are right in supposing that she had her reasons. It came a little hard on the Chancellor of Barodia, but the innocent must needs suffer for the ambitions of the unprincipled—a maxim I borrow from *Euralia Past and Present*; Roger in his moral vein.

"Well," said Merriwig to the Countess, "that's done it."

"It really is war?" asked Belvane.

"It is. Hyacinth is looking for my armour at this moment."

"What did the King of Barodia say?"

"He didn't *say* anything. He wrote 'W A R' in red on a dirty bit of paper, pinned it to my messenger's ear, and sent him back again."

"How very crude," said the Countess.

"Oh, I thought it was—er—rather forcible," said the King awkwardly. Secretly he had admired it a good deal and wished that he had been the one to do it.

"Of course," said the Countess, with a charming smile, "that sort of thing depends so *very* much on who does it. Now from your Majesty it would have seemed—dignified."

"He must have been very angry," said the King, picking up first one and then another of a number of swords which lay in front of him. "I wish I had seen his face when he got my Note."

"So do I," sighed the Countess. She wished it much more than the King. It is the tragedy of writing a good letter that you cannot be there when it is opened: a maxim of my own, the thought never having occurred to Roger Scurvilegs, who was a dull correspondent.

The King was still taking up and putting down his swords.

"It's very awkward," he muttered; "I wonder if Hyacinth . . ." He went to the door and called, "Hyacinth!"

"Coming, Father," called back Hyacinth from a higher floor.

The Countess rose and curtsied deeply.

"Good morning, your Royal Highness."

"Good morning, Countess," said Hyacinth brightly. She liked the Countess (you couldn't help it), but rather wished she didn't.

"Oh, Hyacinth," said the King, "come and tell me about these swords. Which is my magic one?"

Hyacinth looked at him blankly.

"Oh, Father," she said. "I don't know at all. Does it matter very much?"

"My dear child, of course it matters. Supposing I am fighting the King of Barodia and I have my magic sword, then I'm bound to win. Supposing I haven't, then I'm not bound to."

"Supposing you both had magic swords," said Belvane. It was the sort of thing she *would* say.

The King looked up slowly at her and began to revolve the idea in his mind.

"Well, really," he said, "I hadn't thought of that. Upon my word, I . . ." He turned to his daughter. "Hyacinth, what would happen if we both had magic swords?"

"I suppose you'd go on fighting forever," said Hyacinth.

"Or until the magic wore out of one of them," said Belvane innocently.

"There must be something about it somewhere," said the King, whose morning was in danger of being quite spoiled by this new suggestion; "I'd ask the Chancellor to look it up, only he's so busy just now."

"He'd have plenty of time while the combat was going on," said Belvane thoughtfully. Wonderful creature! she saw already the Chancellor hurrying up to announce that the King of Euralia had won, at the very moment when he lay stretched on the ground by a mortal thrust from his adversary.

The King turned to his swords again.

"Well, anyway, I'm going to be sure of *mine*," he said. "Hyacinth, haven't you *any* idea which it is?" He added in rather a hurt voice, "Naturally I left the marking of my swords to *you*."

His daughter examined the swords one by one.

"Here it is," she cried. "It's got *M* on it for *magic*."

"Or *Merriwig*," said the Countess to her diary.

The expression of joy on the King's face at his daughter's discovery had just time to appear and fade away again.

"You are not being very helpful this morning, Countess," he said severely.

Instantly the Countess was on her feet, her diary thrown to the floor—no, never thrown—laid gently on the floor, and herself, hands clasped at her breast, a figure of reproachful penitence before him.

"Oh, your Majesty, forgive me—if your Majesty had only asked me—I didn't know your Majesty wanted me—I thought her Royal Highness . . . But *of course* I'll find your Majesty's sword for you." Did she stroke his head as she said this? I have often wondered. It would be like her impudence, and her motherliness, and her—and, in fact, like her. *Euralia Past and Present* is silent upon the point. Roger Scurvilegs, who had only seen Belvane at the unimpressionable age of two, would have had it against her if he could, so perhaps there is nothing in it.

"There!" she said, and she picked out the magic sword almost at once.

"Then I'll get back to my work," said Hyacinth cheerfully, and left them to each other.

The King, smiling happily, girded on his sword. But a sudden doubt assailed him.

"Are you sure it's the one?"

"Try it on *me*," cried the Countess superbly, falling on her knees and stretching up her arms to him. The toe of her little shoe touched her diary; its presence there uplifted her. Even as she knelt, she saw herself describing the scene. How do you spell *"offered"*? she wondered.

I think the King was already in love with her,
though he found it so difficult to say the decisive words. But even so, he could only have
been in love a week or two; a fortnight in the
last forty years; and he had worn a sword since
he was twelve. In a crisis it is the old love and
not the greater love which wins (Roger's, but I
think I agree with him), and instinctively the
King drew his sword. If it were magic, a scratch
would kill. Now he would know.

Her enemies said that the Countess could not
go pale; she had her faults, but this was not one
of them. She whitened as she saw the King
standing over her with drawn sword. A hundred thoughts chased each other through her
mind. She wondered if the King would be sorry
afterwards; she wondered what the minstrels
would sing of her, and if her diary would ever
be made public; most of all, she wondered why
she had been such a fool, such a melodramatic
fool.

The King came to himself with a sudden start.
Looking slightly ashamed, he put his sword
back in its scabbard, coughed once or twice to
cover his confusion, and held his hand out to
the Countess to assist her to rise.

"Don't be absurd, Countess," he said. "As if
we could spare you at a time like this. Sit down
and let us talk matters over seriously."

A trifle bewildered by the emotions she had

gone through, Belvane sat down, the beloved diary clasped tightly in her arms. Life seemed singularly sweet just then, the only drawback being that the minstrels would not be singing about her after all. Still, one cannot have everything.

The King walked up and down the room as he talked.

"I am going away to fight," he said, "and I leave my dear daughter behind. In my absence, her Royal Highness will of course rule the country. I want her to feel that she can lean upon you, Countess, for advice and support. I know that I can trust you, for you have just given me a great proof of your devotion and courage."

"Oh, your Majesty!" said Belvane deprecatingly, but feeling very glad that it hadn't been wasted.

"Hyacinth is young and inexperienced. She needs a—a—"

"A mother's guiding hand," said Belvane softly.

The King started and looked away. It was really too late to propose now; he had so much to do before the morrow. Better leave it till he came back from the war.

"You will have no official position," he went on hastily, "other than your present one of Mistress of the Robes; but your influence on her will be very great."

The Countess had already decided on this. However, there *is* a look of modest resignation to an unsought duty which is suited to an occasion of this kind, and the Countess had no difficulty in supplying it.

"I will do all that I can, your Majesty, to help—gladly; but will not the Chancellor—"

"The Chancellor will come with me. He is no fighter, but he is good at spells." He looked round to make sure that they were alone, and then went on confidentially, "He tells me that he has discovered in the archives of the palace a Backward Spell of great value. Should he be able to cast this upon the enemy at the first onslaught, he thinks that our heroic army would have no difficulty in advancing."

"But there will be other learned men," said Belvane innocently, "so much more accustomed to affairs than us poor women, so much better able,"—(What nonsense I'm talking, she said to herself)—"to advise her Royal Highness—"

"Men like that," said the King, "I shall want with me also. If I am to invade Barodia properly, I shall need every man in the kingdom. Euralia must be for the time a country of women only." He turned to her with a smile, and said gallantly, "That will be—er . . . It is—er—not—er . . . One may well—er . . ."

It was so obvious from his manner that something complimentary was struggling to the surface of his mind that Belvane felt it would be kinder not to wait for it.

"Oh, your Majesty," she said, "you flatter my poor sex."

"Not at all," said the King, trying to remember what he had said. He held out his hand. "Well, Countess, I have much to do."

"I, too, your Majesty."

She made him a deep curtsy, and clasping tightly the precious diary, withdrew.

The King, who still seemed worried about something, returned to his table and took up his pen. Here Hyacinth discovered him ten minutes later. His table was covered with scraps of paper, and her eyes lighting casually upon one of them, she read these remarkable words:

"In such a land I should be a most contented subject."

She looked at some of the others. They were even shorter:

"That, dear Countess, would be my . . ."

"A country in which even a King . . ."

"Lucky country!"

The last was crossed out and *bad* written against it.

"Whatever are these, Father?" said Hyacinth.

The King jumped up in great confusion.

"Nothing, dear, nothing," he said. "I was just—er . . . Of course I shall have to address my people, and I was just jotting down a few

. . . However, I shan't want them now." He swept them together, screwed them up tight, and dropped them into a basket.

And what became of them? you ask. Did they light the fires of the Palace next morning? Well, now, here's a curious thing. In Chapter X of *Euralia Past and Present* I happened across these words:

"The King and all the men of the land having left to fight the wicked Barodians, Euralia was now a country of women only—*a country in which even a King might be glad to be a subject*."

Now what does this mean? Is it another example of literary theft? I have already had to expose Shelley. Must I now drag into the light of day a still worse plagiarism by Roger Scurvilegs? The wastepaper baskets of the Palace were no doubt open to him, as to so many historians. But should he not have made acknowledgments?

I do not wish to be hard on Roger. That I differ from him on many points of historical fact has already been made plain, and will be made still more plain as my story goes on. But I have a respect for the man; and on some matters, particularly those concerning Prince Udo of Araby's first appearance in Euralia, I have to rely entirely upon him for my information. Moreover, I have never hesitated to give him credit for such of his epigrams as I have introduced into this book, and I like to think that he would be equally punctilious to others. We know his romantic way; no doubt the thought occurred to him independently. Let us put it at that, anyhow.

Belvane, meanwhile, was getting on. The King had drawn his sword on her and she had not flinched. As a reward she was to be the power behind the throne.

"Not necessarily *behind* the throne," said Belvane to herself.

4

The Princess Hyacinth Leaves It to the Countess

IT IS NOW time to introduce Wiggs to you, and I find myself in a difficulty at once.

What *was* Wiggs's position in the Palace?

This story is hard to tell, for I have to piece it together from the narratives of others, and to supply any gaps in their stories from my knowledge of how the different characters might be expected to act. Perhaps, therefore, it is a good moment in which to introduce to you the authorities upon whom I rely.

First and foremost, of course, comes Roger Scurvilegs. His monumental work, *Euralia Past and Present*, in seventeen volumes, towers upon my desk as I write. By the merest chance I picked it up (in a metaphorical sense) at that little shop near—I forget its name, but it's the third bookshop on the left as you come into London from the New Barnet end. Upon him I depend for the broad lines of my story, and I have already indicated my opinion of the value of his work.

Secondly, come the many legends and ballads handed on to me years ago by my aunt by marriage, one of the Cornish Smallnoses. She claims to be a direct descendant of that Henry Smallnose whose lucky shot brought about the events which I am to describe. I say she claims to be, and one cannot doubt a lady's word in these matters; certainly she used to speak about Henry with that mixture of pride and extreme familiarity which comes best from a relation. In all matters not touching Henry, I feel that I can rely upon her; in its main lines her narrative is strictly confirmed by Scurvilegs, and she brought to it a picturesqueness and an appreciation of the true character of Belvane which is lacking in the other; but her attitude toward Henry Smallnose was absurd. Indeed, she would have had him the hero of the story. This makes Roger and myself smile. We give him credit for the first shot, and then we drop him.

Thirdly, Belvane herself. Women like Belvane never die, and I met her (or a reincarnation of her) at a country house in Shropshire last summer. I forget what she calls herself now, but I recognized her at once; and, as I watched her, the centuries rolled away and she and I were in Euralia, that pleasant country, together. "Stayed to tea and was very charming." Would she have said that of me, I wonder? But I'm getting sentimental—Roger's great fault.

These then are my authorities; I consult them, and I ask myself, What was Wiggs?

Roger speaks of her simply as an attendant upon the Princess. Now we know that the Princess was seventeen; Wiggs then would be about the same age—a lady in waiting—perhaps even a little older. Why not? you say. The Lady Wiggs, maid of honour to her Royal Highness the Princess Hyacinth, eighteen and a bit, tall and stately. Since she is to endanger Belvane's plans, let her be something of a match for the wicked woman.

Yes, but you would never talk like that if you had heard one of my aunt's stories. Nor if you had seen Belvane would you think that any grown-up woman could be a match for her.

Wiggs was a child; I feel it in my bones. In all the legends and ballads handed down to me by my aunt, she appears to me as a little girl— Alice in a fairy story. Roger or no Roger, I must have her a child.

And even Roger cannot keep up the farce that she is a real lady in waiting. In one place he tells us that she dusts the throne of the Princess; can you see her ladyship, eighteen last February, doing that? At other times he allows her to take orders from the Countess; I ask you to imagine a maid of honour taking orders from any but her own mistress. Conceive her dignity!

A little friend, then, of Hyacinth's, let us say; ready to do anything for anybody who loved, or appeared to love, her mistress.

The King had departed for the wars. His magic sword girded to his side, his cloak of darkness, not worn but rolled up behind him, lest the absence of his usual extensive shadow should disturb his horse, he rode at the head of his men to meet the enemy. Hyacinth had seen him off from the Palace steps. Five times he had come back to give her his last instructions, and a sixth time for his sword, but now he was gone, and she was alone on the castle walls with Wiggs.

"Saying goodbye to fathers is very tiring," said Hyacinth. "I do hope he'll be all right. Wiggs, although we oughtn't to mention it to anybody, and although he's only just gone, we do think it will be rather fun being Queen, don't we?"

"It must be lovely," said Wiggs, gazing at her with large eyes. "Can you really do whatever you like now?"

Hyacinth nodded.

"I always *did* whatever I liked," she said, "but now I really *can* do it."

"Could you cut anybody's head off?"

"Easily," said the Princess confidently.

"I should hate to cut anybody's head off."

"So should I, Wiggs. Let's decide to have no heads off just at present—till we're more used to it."

Wiggs still kept her eyes fixed upon the Princess.

"Which is stronger," she asked, "you or a Fairy?"

"I knew you were going to ask something horrid like that," said Hyacinth, pretending to be angry. She looked quickly round to see that nobody was listening, and then whispered in Wiggs's ear, "I am."

"O—oh!" said Wiggs. "How lovely!"

"Isn't it? Did you ever hear the story of Father and the Fairy?"

"His Majesty?"

"His Majesty the King of Euralia. It happened in the forest one day just after he became King."

Did *you* ever hear the story? I expect not.

Well, then, you must hear it. But there will be too many inverted commas in it if I let Hyacinth tell you, so I shall tell you myself.

It was just after he became King. He was so proud that he used to go about saying, "I am the King. I am the King." And sometimes, "The King am I. The King I am." He was saying this one day in the forest when a Fairy overheard him. So she appeared in front of him and said, "I believe you are the King?"

"I am the King," said Merriwig. "I am the King, I am the—"

"And yet," said the Fairy, "what is a King after all?"

"It is a very powerful thing to be a King," said Merriwig proudly.

"Supposing I were to turn you into a—a small sheep. Then where would you be?"

The King thought anxiously for a moment.

"I should like to be a small sheep," he said.

The Fairy waved her wand.

"Then you can be one," she said, "until you own that a Fairy is much more powerful than a King."

So all at once he was a small sheep.

"Well?" said the Fairy.

"Well?" said the King.

"Which is more powerful, a King or a Fairy?"

"A King," said Merriwig. "Besides being more woolly," he added.

There was silence for a little. Merriwig began to eat some grass.

"I don't think much of Fairies," he said with his mouth full. "I don't think they're very powerful."

The Fairy looked at him angrily.

"They can't make you say things you don't want to say," he explained.

The Fairy stamped her foot.

"Be a toad," she said, waving her wand. "A nasty, horrid, crawling toad."

"I've *always* wanted—" began Merriwig, "—to be a toad," he ended from lower down.

"Well?" said the Fairy.

"I don't think much of Fairies," said the King. "I don't think they're very powerful." He waited for the Fairy to look at him, but she pretended to be thinking of something else. After waiting a minute or two, he added, "They can't make you say things you don't want to say."

The Fairy stamped her foot still more angrily, and moved her wand a third time.

"Be silent!" she commanded. "And stay silent forever!"

There was no sound in the forest. The Fairy looked at the blue sky through the green roof above her; she looked through the tall trunks of the trees to the King's castle beyond; her eyes fell upon the little glade on her left, upon the mossy bank on her right . . . but she would not look down to the toad at her feet.

No, she wouldn't. . . .

She *wouldn't*. . . .

And yet—

It was too much for her. She could resist no longer. She looked at the nasty, horrid, crawling toad, the dumb toad at her feet that was once a King.

And, catching her eye, the toad—*winked*.

Some winks are more expressive than others. The Fairy knew quite well what this one meant. It meant:

"I don't think much of Fairies. I don't think they're very powerful. They can't make you say things you don't want to say."

The Fairy waved her wand in disgust.

"Oh, be a King again," she said impatiently, and vanished.

And so that is the story of how the King of Euralia met the Fairy in the forest. Roger Scurvilegs tells it well—indeed, almost as well as I do—but he burdens it with a moral. You must think it out for yourself; I shall not give it to you.

Wiggs didn't bother about the moral. Her elbows on her knees, her chin resting on her hands, she gazed at the forest and imagined the scene to herself.

How wonderful to be a King like that! she thought.

"That was a long time ago," explained Hyacinth. "Father must have been rather lovely in those days," she added.

"It was a very bad Fairy," said Wiggs.

"It was a very stupid one. I wouldn't have given in to Father like that."

"But there are good Fairies, aren't there? I met one once."

"You, child? Where?"

I don't know if it would have made any difference to Euralian history if Wiggs had been allowed to tell about her Fairy then; as it was, she didn't tell the story till later on, when Belvane happened to be near. I regret to say that Belvane listened. It was the sort of story that *always* got overheard, she explained afterwards, as if that were any excuse. On this occasion she was just too early to overhear, but in time to prevent the story being told without her.

"The Countess Belvane," said an attendant, and her ladyship made a superb entry.

"Good morning, Countess," said Hyacinth.

"Good morning, your Royal Highness. Ah, Wiggs, sweet child," she added carelessly, putting out a hand to pat the sweet child's head, but missing it.

"Wiggs was just telling me a story," said the Princess.

"Sweet child," said Belvane, feeling vaguely for her with the other hand. "*Could* I interrupt the story with a little business, your Royal Highness?"

At a nod from the Princess, Wiggs withdrew.

"Well?" said Hyacinth nervously.

Belvane had always a curious effect on the Princess when they were alone together. There was something about her large manner which made Hyacinth feel like a schoolgirl who has been behaving badly: alarmed and apologetic. I feel like this myself when I have an interview with my publishers, and Roger Scurvilegs (upon the same subject) drags in a certain uncle of his before whom (so he says) he always appears at his worst. It is a common experience.

"Just one or two little schemes to submit to your Majesty," said the Countess. "How silly of me—I mean, your Royal Highness. Of course your Royal Highness may not like them at all, but in case your Royal Highness did, I just— well, I just wrote them out."

She unfolded, one by one, a series of ornamental parchments.

"They are beautifully written," said the Princess.

Belvane blushed at the compliment. She had a passion for coloured inks and rulers. In her diary the day of the week was always underlined in red, the important words in the day's doings being frequently picked out in gold. On taking up the diary, you saw at once that you were in the presence of somebody.

The first parchment was headed:

SCHEME FOR ECONOMY IN REALM

Economy caught the eye in pale pink.
The next parchment was headed:

SCHEME FOR SAFETY OF REALM

Safety clamoured to you in blue.
The third parchment was headed:

SCHEME FOR ENCOURAGEMENT OF LITERATURE IN REALM

Encouragement of Literature had got rather cramped in the small quarters available for it. A heading, Belvane felt, should be in one line; she had started in letters too big for it, and the fact that the green ink was giving out made it impossible to start afresh.

There were ten parchments altogether.

By the end of the third one, the Princess began to feel uncomfortable.

By the end of the fifth one she knew that it was a mistake her ever having come into the Royal Family at all.

By the end of the seventh she decided that if the Countess would forgive her this time she would never be naughty again.

By the end of the ninth one she was just going to cry.

The tenth one was in a very loud orange and was headed:

SCHEME FOR ASSISTING CALISTHENICS IN REALM

"Yes," said the Princess faintly; "I think it would be a good idea."

"I thought if your Royal Highness approved," said Belvane, "we might just—"

Hyacinth felt herself blushing guiltily—she couldn't think why.

"I leave it to you, Countess," she murmured. "I am sure you know best."

It was a remark which she would never have made to her father.

5

Belvane Indulges Her Hobby

IN A GLADE in the forest the Countess Belvane was sitting: her throne, a fallen log, her courtiers, that imaginary audience which was always with her. For once in her life she was nervous; she had an anxious morning in front of her.

I can tell you the reason at once. Her Royal Highness was going to review her Royal Highness's Army of Amazons (see *Scheme II*, *Safety of Realm*). In half an hour she would be here.

And why not? you say. Could anything be more gratifying?

I will tell you why not. There was no Army of Amazons. In order that her Royal Highness should not know the sad truth, Belvane drew their pay for them. 'Twas better thus.

In any trouble Belvane comforted herself by reading up her diary. She undid the enormous volume, and, idly turning the pages, read some of the more delightful extracts to herself.

"Monday, June first," she read. "Became bad."

She gave a sigh of resignation to the necessity of being bad. Roger Scurvilegs is of the opinion that she might have sighed a good many years before. According to him she was born bad.

"Tuesday, June second," she read on. "Realized in the privacy of my heart that I was destined to rule the country. *Wednesday, June third.* Decided to oust the Princess. *Thursday, June fourth.* Began ousting."

What a confession for any woman—even for one who had become bad last Monday! No wonder Belvane's diary was not for everybody. Let us look over her shoulder and read some more of the wicked woman's confessions.

"Friday, June fifth. Made myself a . . ." Oh, that's quite private. However, we may read this: *"Thought for the week.* Beware lest you should tumble down In reaching for another's crown." An admirable sentiment which Roger Scurvilegs would have approved, though he could not have rhymed it so neatly.

The Countess turned on a few more pages and prepared to write up yesterday's events.

"Tuesday, June twenty-third," she said to herself. "Now what happened? Acclaimed with enthusiasm outside the Palace—how do you spell *enthusiasm?"* She bit the end of her pencil and

pondered. She turned back the pages till she came to the place.

"Yes," she said thoughtfully. "It had three *s*'s last time, so it's *z*'s turn."

She wrote *enthuzziazm* lightly in pencil; later on it would be picked out in gold.

She closed the diary hastily. Somebody was coming.

It was Wiggs.

"Oh, if you please, your Ladyship, her Royal Highness sent me to tell you that she would be here at eleven o'clock to review her new army."

It was the last thing of which Belvane wanted reminding.

"Ah, Wiggs, sweet child," she said, "you find me overwhelmed." She gave a tragic sigh. "Leader of the Corps de Ballet"—she indicated with her toe how this was done—"Commander-in-Chief of the Army of Amazons"—here she saluted, and it was certainly the least she could do for the money—"Warden of the Antimacassars and Grand Mistress of the Robes, I have a busy life. Just come and dust this log for her Royal Highness. All this work wears me out, Wiggs, but it is my duty and I do it."

"Woggs says you make a very good thing out of it," said Wiggs innocently as she began to dust. "It must be nice to make very good things out of things."

The Countess looked coldly at her. It is one

thing to confide to your diary that you are bad, it's quite another to have Woggseses shouting it out all over the country.

"I don't know what Woggs is," said Belvane sternly, "but send it to me at once."

As soon as Wiggs was gone, Belvane gave herself up to her passions. She strode up and down the velvety sward, saying to herself, "Bother! Bother! Bother! Bother!" Her outbreak of violence over, she sat gloomily down on the log and abandoned herself to despair. Her hair fell in two plaits down her back to her waist; on second thought she arranged them in front—if one is going to despair, one may as well do it to the best advantage.

Suddenly a thought struck her.

"I am alone," she said. "Dare I soliloquize? I will. It is a thing I have not done for weeks. 'Oh, what a . . .'" She got up quickly. "*Nobody* could soliloquize on a log like that," she said crossly. She decided she could do it just as effectively when standing. With one pale hand raised to the skies she began again.

"Oh, what a—"

"Did you call me, Mum?" said Woggs, appearing suddenly.

"*Bother!*" said Belvane. She gave a shrug of resignation. "Another time," she told herself. She turned to Woggs.

Woggs must have been quite close at hand to

have been found by Wiggs so quickly, and I suspect her of playing in the forest when she ought to have been doing her lessons, or mending the stockings, or whatever made up her day's work. Woggs I find nearly as difficult to explain as Wiggs; it is a terrible thing for an author to have a lot of people running about his book without any invitation from him at all. However, since Woggs is there, we must make the best of her. I fancy that she was a year or two younger than Wiggs and of rather inferior education. Witness her low innuendo about the Lady Belvane, and the fact that she called a Countess "Mum."

"Come here," said Belvane. "Are you what they call Woggs?"

"Please, Mum," said Woggs nervously.

The Countess winced at the "Mum," but went on bravely. "What have you been saying about me?"

"N—nothing, Mum."

Belvane winced again, and said, "Do you know what I do to little girls who say things about me? I cut their heads off; I"—she tried to think of something very alarming!—"I—I stop their jam for tea. I—I am *most* annoyed with them."

Woggs suddenly saw what a wicked thing she had done.

"Oh, please, Mum," she said brokenly, and fell on her knees.

"Don't call me 'Mum,' " burst out Belvane. "It's so *ugly*. Why do you suppose I ever wanted to be a countess at all, Woggs, if it wasn't so as not to be called 'Mum' any more?"

"I don't know, Mum," said Woggs.

Belvane gave it up. The whole morning was going wrong anyhow.

"Come here, child"—she sighed—"and listen. You have been a very naughty girl, but I'm going to let you off this time, and in return I've something you are going to do for me."

"Yes, Mum," said Woggs.

Belvane barely shuddered now. A sudden brilliant plan had come to her.

"Her Royal Highness is about to review her Army of Amazons. It is a sudden idea of her Royal Highness's, and it comes at an unfortunate moment, for it so happens that the Army is—er . . ." *What* was the Army doing? Ah, yes "—maneuvering in a distant part of the country. But we must not disappoint her Royal Highness. What then shall we do, Woggs?"

"I don't know, Mum," said Woggs stolidly.

Not having expected any real assistance from her, the Countess went on, "I will tell you. You see yonder tree? Armed to the teeth, *you* will march round and round it, giving the impression to one on this side of a large army passing. For this you will be rewarded. Here is . . ." She felt in the bag she carried. "No, on second thought, I will owe it to you. Now you quite understand?"

"Yes, Mum," said Woggs.

"Very well, then. Run along to the Palace and get a sword and a helmet and a bow and an arrow and an—an arrow and anything you like, and then come back here and wait behind those bushes. When I clap my hands, the army will begin to march."

Woggs curtsied and ran off.

It is probable that at this point the Countess would have resumed her soliloquy, but we shall never know, for the next moment the Princess and her Court were seen approaching from the other end of the glade. Belvane advanced to meet them.

"Good morning, your Royal Highness," she said, "a beautiful day, is it not?"

"Beautiful, Countess."

With the Court at her back, Hyacinth for the moment was less nervous than usual, but almost at the first words of the Countess she felt her self-confidence oozing from her. Did I say I was like this with my publishers? And Roger's dragged-in uncle—one can't explain it.

The Court stood about in picturesque attitudes while Belvane went on:

"Your Royal Highness's brave Women Defenders, the Home Defense Army of Amazons" (here she saluted; one soon gets into the knack of it, and it gives an air of efficiency) "have looked forward to this day for weeks. How their hearts fill with pride at the thought of being reviewed by your Royal Highness!"

She had paid, or rather received, the money for the Army so often that she had quite got to believe in its existence. She even kept a roll of the different companies (it meant more delightful red ink, for one thing), and wrote herself little notes recommending Corporal Gretal Hottshott for promotion to sergeant.

"I know very little about armies, I'm afraid," said Hyacinth. "I've always left that to my father. But I think it's a sweet idea of yours to enroll the women to defend me. It's a little expensive, is it not?"

"Your Royal Highness, armies are *always* expensive."

The Princess took her seat, and beckoned Wiggs with a smile to her side. The Court, in attitudes even more picturesque than before, grouped itself behind her.

"Is your Royal Highness ready?"

"Quite ready, Countess."

The Countess clapped her hands.

There was a moment's hesitation, and then, armed to the teeth, Amazon after Amazon marched by. . . .

An impressive scene. . . .

However, Wiggs must needs try to spoil it.

"Why, it's Woggs!" she cried.

"Silly child!" said Belvane in an undertone, giving her a push.

The Princess looked round inquiringly.

"The absurd creature," explained the Countess, "thought she recognized a friend in your Royal Highness's gallant Army."

"How clever of her! They all look exactly alike to *me*."

Belvane was equal to the occasion.

"The uniform and discipline of an army have that effect, rather," she said. "It has often been noticed."

"I suppose so," said the Princess vaguely. "Oughtn't they to march in fours? I seem to remember, when I came to reviews with Father—"

"Ah, your Royal Highness, that was an army of men. With women—well, we found that if they marched side by side, they *would* talk all the time."

The Court, which had been resting on the right leg with the left knee bent, now rested on the left leg with the right knee bent. Woggs also was getting tired. The last company of the Army of Amazons was not marching with the abandon of the first company.

"I think I should like them to halt now so that I can address them," said Hyacinth.

Belvane was taken aback for the moment.

"I am afraid, your—your Royal Highness,"

she stammered, her brain working busily all the time, "that that would be contrary to—to—to the spirit of—er—the King's Regulations. An army—an army in marching order—must—er—*march.*" She made a long forward movement with her hand. "Must march," she repeated, with an innocent smile.

"I see," said Hyacinth, blushing guiltily again.

Belvane gave a loud cough. The last veteran but two of the Army looked inquiringly at her and passed. The last veteran but one came in and was greeted with a still louder cough. Rather tentatively the last veteran of all entered and met such an unmistakable frown that it was obvious that the march-past was over. . . . Woggs took off her helmet and rested in the bushes.

"That is all, your Royal Highness," said Belvane. "One hundred and fifty-eight marched past, two hundred and seventeen reported sick, making six hundred and twenty-two; nine are on guard at the Palace—six hundred and thirty-two and nine make eight hundred and fifteen. Add twenty-eight under age, and we bring it up to the round thousand."

Wiggs opened her mouth to say something, but decided that her mistress would probably wish to say it instead. Hyacinth, however, merely looked unhappy.

Belvane came a little nearer.

"I—er—forgot if I mentioned to your Royal Highness that we are paying out today. One silver piece a day and several days in the week, multiplied by—how many did I say?—comes to ten thousand pieces of gold." She produced a document, beautifully ruled. "If your Royal Highness would kindly initial here . . ."

Mechanically the Princess signed.

"Thank you, your Royal Highness. And now perhaps I had better go and see about it at once."

She curtsied deeply, and then, remembering her position, saluted and marched off.

Now Roger Scurvilegs would see her go without a pang; he would then turn over to his next chapter, beginning "Meanwhile the King . . ." and leave you under the impression that the Countess Belvane was a common thief. I am no such chronicler as that. At all costs I will be fair to my characters.

Belvane, then, had a weakness. She had several of which I have already told you, but this was another one. She had a passion for the distribution of largesse.

I know an old gentleman who plays bowls every evening. He trundles his skip (or whatever he calls it) to one end of the green, toddles after it, and trundles it back again. Think of him for a moment, and then think of Belvane on her cream-white palfrey, tossing a bag of gold to right of her and flinging a bag of gold to left of her as she rides through the cheering crowds; upon my word I think hers is the more admirable exercise.

And, I assure you, no less exacting. When once one has got into this habit of "flinging" or "tossing" money, to give it in any ordinary way, to slide it gently into the palm, is unbearable. Which of us who has, in a heroic moment, flung half a crown to a cabman can ever be content afterwards to hold out a handful of threepenny bits and coppers to him? One must always be flinging. . . .

So it was with Belvane. The largesse habit had got hold of her. It is an expensive habit, but her way of doing it was less expensive than most. The people were taxed to pay for the Amazon Army; the pay of the Amazon Army was flung back at them; could anything be fairer?

True, it brought her admiration and applause. But what woman does not like admiration? Is that an offense? If it is, it is something very different from the common theft of which Roger Scurvilegs would accuse her. Let us be fair.

6

There Are No Wizards in Barodia

MEANWHILE "THE KING of Euralia was prosecuting the war with the utmost vigour."

So says Roger in that famous chapter of his, and certainly Merriwig was very busy.

On the declaration of war the Euralian forces, in accordance with custom, had marched into Barodia. However hot ran the passion between them, the two Kings always preserved the elementary courtesies of war. The last battle had taken place in Euralian territory; this time, therefore, Barodia was the scene of the conflict. To Barodia, then, King Merriwig led his army. Suitable pasture land had been allotted them as a camping ground, and amid the cheers of the Barodian populace the Euralians made their simple preparations for the night.

The two armies had now been sitting opposite to each other for some weeks, but neither side had been idle. On the very first morning Merriwig had put on his Cloak of Darkness and gone to the enemy's camp to explore the situation. Unfortunately, the same idea had occurred at the same moment to the King of Barodia. He also had his Cloak of Darkness.

Halfway across, to the utmost astonishment of both, the two Kings had come violently into contact. Realizing that they had met some unprecedented enchantment, they had hurried home after the recoil to consult their respective Chancellors. The Chancellors could make nothing of it. They could only advise their Majesties to venture another attempt on the following morning.

"But by a different route," said the Chancellors, "whereby the Magic Pillar shall be avoided."

So by the more southerly path the two Kings ventured out next morning. Halfway across there was another violent collision, and both Kings sat down suddenly to think it out.

"Wonder of wonders," said Merriwig. "There is a magic wall stretching between the two armies."

He stood up and, holding up his hand, said impressively:

> "Bo, boll, bill, bole.
> Wo, woll—"

"Mystery of mysteries!" cried the King of Barodia. "It can . . ."

He stopped suddenly. Both Kings coughed. They were remembering with some shame their fright of yesterday.

"Who are you?" said the King of Barodia.

Merriwig saw that there was need to dissemble.

"His Majesty's swineherd," he said, in what he imagined might be a swineherd's voice.

"Er—so am I," said the King of Barodia, rather feebly.

There was obviously nothing for it but for them to discuss swine.

Merriwig was comfortably ignorant of the subject. The King of Barodia knew rather less than that.

"Er—how many have you?" asked the latter.

"Seven thousand," said Merriwig at random.

"Er—so have I," said the King of Barodia, still more feebly.

"Couples," explained Merriwig.

"Mine are ones," said the King of Barodia, determined to be independent at last.

Each King was surprised to find how easy it was to talk to an expert on his own subject. The King of Barodia, indeed, began to feel reckless.

"Well," he said, "I must be getting back. It's—er—milking time."

"So must I," said Merriwig. "By the way," he added, "what do you feed yours on?"

The King of Barodia was not quite sure if it was apple sauce or not. He decided that perhaps it wasn't.

"That's a secret," he said darkly. "Been handed down from generation to generation."

Merriwig could think of nothing better to say to this than "Ah!" He said it very impressively, and with a word of farewell, returned to his camp.

He was in brilliant form over the wassail bowl that night as he drew a picture of his triumphant dissimulation. It is only fair to say that the King of Barodia was in brilliant form too. . . .

For several weeks after this the battle raged. Sometimes the whole Euralian army would line up outside its camp and call upon the Barodians to fight; at other times the Barodian army would form fours in full view of the Euralians in the hope of provoking a conflict. At intervals the two Chancellors would look up old spells, scour the country for wizards, or send each other insulting messages. At the end of a month it was difficult to say which side had obtained the advantage.

A little hill surmounted by a single tree lay halfway between the two camps. Thither one fine morning came the two Kings and the two Chancellors on bloody business bent. (The phrase is Roger's). Their object was nothing less than to arrange that personal fight between the two monarchs which was always a feature of Barodo-Euralian warfare. The two Kings having shaken hands, their Chancellors proceeded to settle the details.

"I suppose," said the Chancellor of Barodia, "that your Majesties will wish to fight with swords?"

"Certainly," said the King of Barodia promptly; so promptly that Merriwig felt certain that he had a Magic Sword, too.

"Cloaks of Darkness are not allowed, of course," said the Chancellor of Euralia.

"Why, have *you* got one?" said each King quickly to the other.

Merriwig was the first to recover himself.

"I have one—naturally," he said. "It's a curious thing that the only one of my subjects who has one is my—er—swineherd."

"That's funny," said the King of Barodia. "My swineherd has one, too."

"Of course," said Merriwig, "they are almost a necessity to swineherding."

"Particularly in the milking season," said the King of Barodia.

They looked at each other with added respect. Not many Kings in those days had the technicalities of such a humble trade at their fingers' ends.

The Chancellor of Barodia had been referring to the precedents.

"It was after the famous conflict between the two grandfathers of your Majesties that the use of the Magic Cloak in personal combats was discontinued."

"Great-grandfathers," said the Chancellor of Euralia.

"Grandfathers, I think."

"Great-grandfathers, if I am not mistaken."

Their tempers were rising rapidly, and the Chancellor of Barodia was just about to give the Chancellor of Euralia a push when Merriwig intervened.

"Never mind about that," he said impatiently. "Tell us what happened when our—our ancestors fought."

"It happened in this way, your Majesty. Your Majesty's grandfather—"

"Great-grandfather," said a small voice.

The Chancellor cast one bitter look at his opponent and went on:

"The ancestors of your two Majesties arranged to settle the war of that period by personal combat. The two armies were drawn up in full array. In front of them the two monarchs shook hands. Drawing their swords and casting their Magic Cloaks around them, they—"

"Well?" said Merriwig eagerly.

"It is rather a painful story, your Majesty."

"Go on, I shan't mind."

"Well, your Majesty, drawing their swords

and casting their Magic Cloaks around them, they—h'r'm—returned to the wassail bowl."

"Dear, dear," said Merriwig.

"When the respective armies, who had been waiting eagerly the whole of the afternoon for some result of the combat, returned to camp, they found their Majesties—"

"Asleep," said the Chancellor of Euralia hastily.

"Asleep," agreed the Chancellor of Barodia. "The excuse of their two Majesties that they had suddenly forgotten the day, though naturally accepted at the time, was deemed inadequate by later historians." (By Roger and myself, anyway.)

Some further details were discussed, and then the conference closed. The great fight was fixed for the following morning.

The day broke fine. At an early hour Merriwig was up and practising thrusts upon a suspended pillow. At intervals he would consult a little book entitled *Swordplay for Sovereigns*, and then return to his pillow. At breakfast he was nervous but talkative. After breakfast he wrote a tender letter to Hyacinth and a still more tender one to the Countess Belvane, and burned them. He repeated his little rhyme, "Bo, boll, bill, bole," several times to himself until he was word perfect. It was just possible that it might be useful. His last thoughts as he rode on to the field were of his great-grandfather. Without admiring him, he quite saw his point.

The fight was a brilliant one. First Merriwig aimed a blow at the King of Barodia's head which the latter parried. Then the King of Barodia aimed a blow at his adversary's head which Merriwig parried. This went on three or four times, and then Merriwig put into practice a remarkable trick which the Captain of his Bodyguard had taught him. It was his turn to parry, but instead of doing this, he struck again at his opponent's head; and if the latter in sheer surprise had not stumbled and fallen, there might have been a very serious ending to the affair.

Noon found them still at it; cut and parry, cut and parry; at each stroke the opposing armies roared their applause. When darkness put an end to the conflict, honours were evenly divided.

It was a stiff but proud King of Euralia who received the congratulations of his subjects that night; so proud that he had to pour out his heart to somebody. He wrote to his daughter.

"My Dear Hyacinth,

"You will be glad to hear that your father is going on well and that Euralia is as determined as ever to uphold its honour and dignity. Today I fought the King of Barodia, and considering that, most unfairly, he was using a Magic Sword, I think I may say that I did well. The Countess Belvane will be interested to hear that I made 4,638 strokes at my opponent and parried 4,637 strokes from him. This is good for a man of my age. Do you remember that magic ointment my aunt used to give me? Have we any of it left?

"I played a very clever trick the other day by pretending to be a swineherd. I talked to a real one I met for quite a long time about swine without his suspecting me. The Countess might be interested to hear this. It would have been very awkward for me if it had been found out who I was.

"I hope you are getting along all right. Do you consult the Countess Belvane at all? I think she would be able to advise you in any difficulties. A young girl needs a guiding hand, and I think the Countess would be able to advise you in any difficulties. Do you consult her at all?

"I am afraid this is going to be a long war. There doesn't seem to be a wizard in the country at all, and without one, it is a little difficult to know how to go on. I say my spell every now and then—you remember the one:

> 'Bo, boll, bill, bole.
> Wo, woll, will, wole.'

and it certainly keeps off dragons, but we don't

seem to get any nearer defeating the enemy's army. You might tell the Countess Belvane that about my spell; she would be interested.

"Tomorrow I go on with my fight with the King of Barodia. I feel quite confident now that I can hold him. He parries well, but his cutting is not very good. I am glad the Countess found my sword for me; tell her that it has been most useful.

"I must now close as I must go to bed so as to be ready for my fight tomorrow. Goodbye, dear. I am always,

Your Loving Father

"P.S. I hope you are not finding your position too difficult. If you are in any difficulties you should consult the Countess Belvane. I think she would be able to advise you. Don't forget about that ointment. Perhaps the Countess might know about some other kind. It's for stiffness. I am afraid this is going to be a long war."

The King sealed up the letter and dispatched it by special messenger the next morning. It came to Hyacinth at a critical moment. We shall see in the next chapter what effect it had upon her.

7

The Princess Receives a Letter and Writes One

THE PRINCESS HYACINTH came in from her morning's ride in a very bad temper. She went straight up to her favourite seat on the castle walls and sent for Wiggs.

"Wiggs," she said, "what's the matter with me?"

Wiggs looked puzzled. She had been dusting the books in the library; and when you dust books you simply *must* stop every now and then to take just one little peep inside, and then you look inside another one and another one, and by the time you have finished dusting, your head is so full of things you have seen that you have to be asked questions very slowly indeed.

"I'm pretty, aren't I?" went on Hyacinth.

That was an easy one.

"Lovely!" said Wiggs, with a deep breath.

"And I'm not unkind to anybody?"

"Unkind!" said Wiggs indignantly.

"Then why—oh, Wiggs, I know it's silly of me, but it *hurts* me that my people are so much fonder of the Countess than of me."

"Oh, I'm sure they're not, your Royal Highness."

"Well, they cheer her much louder than they cheer me."

Wiggs tried to think of a way of comforting her mistress, but her head was still full of the last book she had dusted.

"Why should they be so fond of her?" demanded Hyacinth.

"Perhaps because she's so funny," said Wiggs.

"Funny! Is she funny?" said the Princess coldly. "She doesn't make *me* laugh."

"Well, it *was* funny of her to make Woggs march round and round that tree like that, *wasn't* it?"

"Like what? You don't mean . . ." The Princess's eyes were wide open with astonishment. "Was that Woggs all the time?"

"Yes, your Royal Highness. Wasn't it lovely and funny of her?"

The Princess looked across to the forest and nodded to herself.

"Yes. That's it. Wiggs, I don't believe there has ever been an Army at all. . . . And I pay them every week!" She added solemnly, "There are moments when I don't believe that woman is quite honest."

"Do you mean she isn't good?" asked Wiggs in awe.

Hyacinth nodded.

"I'm *never* good," said Wiggs firmly.

"What do you mean, silly? You're the best little girl in Euralia."

"I'm *not*. I do awful things sometimes. Do you know what I did yesterday?"

"Something terrible!" Hyacinth smiled.

"I tore my apron."

"You baby! That isn't being bad," said Hyacinth absently. She was still thinking of that awful review.

"The Countess says it is."

"The Countess?"

"Do you know why I want to be *very* good?" said Wiggs, coming up close to the Princess.

"Why dear?"

"Because then I could dance like a fairy."

"Is that how it's done?" asked the Princess, rather amused. "The Countess must dance *very* heavily." She suddenly remembered something and added, "Why, of course, child, you were going to tell me about a fairy you met, weren't you? That was weeks ago, though. Tell me now. It will help me to forget things which make me rather angry."

It was a simple little story. There must have

been many like it in the books which Wiggs had been dusting; but these were simple times, and the oldest story always seemed new.

Wiggs had been by herself in the forest. A baby rabbit had run past her, terrified, a ferret in pursuit. Wiggs had picked the little fluffy thing up in her arms and comforted it; the ferret had slowed down, walked past very indifferently with its hands, as it were, in its pockets, hesitated a moment, and then remembered an important letter which it had forgotten to post. Wiggs was left alone with the baby rabbit, and before she knew where she was, the rabbit was gone and there was a fairy in front of her.

"You have saved my life," said the fairy. "That was a wicked magician after me, and if he had caught me then, he would have killed me."

"Please, your Fairiness, I didn't know fairies *could* die," said Wiggs.

"They can when they take on animal shape or human shape. He could not hurt me now, but before . . ." She shuddered.

"I'm so glad you're all right now," said Wiggs politely.

"Thanks to you, my child. I must reward you. Take this ring. When you have been good for a whole day, you can have one good wish; when you have been bad for a whole day, you can have one bad wish. One good wish and one bad wish—that is all it will allow anybody to have."

With these words she vanished and left Wiggs alone with the ring.

So, ever after that, Wiggs tried desperately hard to be good and have the good wish, but it was difficult work. Something always went wrong; she tore her apron or read books when she ought to have been dusting, or . . . Well, you or I would probably have given it up at once, and devoted ourselves to earning the bad wish. But Wiggs was a nice little girl.

"And, oh I *do* so want to be good," said Wiggs earnestly to the Princess, "so that I could wish to dance like a fairy." She had a sudden anxiety. "That *is* a good wish, *isn't* it?"

"It's a lovely wish; but I'm sure you could dance now if you tried."

"I can't," said Wiggs. "I always dance like this."

She jumped up and danced a few steps. Wiggs was a dear little girl, but her dancing reminded you of a very dusty road going uphill all the way, with nothing but suet puddings waiting for you on the top. Something like that.

"It isn't *really* graceful, is it?" she said candidly, as she came to rest.

"Well, I suppose the fairies *do* dance better than that."

"So that's why I want to be good, so as I can have my wish."

"I really must see this ring," said the Princess. "It sounds fascinating." She looked coldly in front of her and added, "Good morning, Countess." (How long had the woman been there?)

"Good morning, your Royal Highness. I ventured to come up unannounced. Ah, sweet child." She waved a caressing hand at Wiggs.

(Even if she had overheard anything, it had only been child's talk.)

"What is it?" asked the Princess. She took a firm hold of the arms of her chair. She would *not, not, not* give way to the Countess this time.

"The merest matter of business, your Royal Highness. Just this scheme for the Encouragement of Literature. Your Royal Highness very wisely decided that in the absence of the men on the sterner business of fighting it was the part of us women to encourage the gentler arts; and for this purpose . . . there was some talk of a competition, and—eh—"

"Ah, yes," said Hyacinth nervously. "I will look into that tomorrow."

"A competition," said Belvane, gazing vaguely over Hyacinth's head. "Some sort of a money prize," she added, as if in a trance.

"There should certainly be some sort of a prize," agreed the Princess. (Why not, she asked herself, if one is to encourage literature?)

"Bags of gold," murmured Belvane to herself. "Bags and bags of gold. Big bags of silver and little bags of gold." She saw herself tossing them to the crowd.

"Well, we'll go into that tomorrow," said Hyacinth hastily.

"I have it all drawn up here," said Belvane. "Your Royal Highness has only to sign. It saves *so* much trouble," she added with a disarming smile. . . . She held the document out—all in the most beautiful colours.

Mechanically the Princess signed.

"Thank you, your Royal Highness." She smiled again, and added, "And now perhaps I had better see about it at once." The Guardian of Literature took a dignified farewell of her Sovereign and withdrew.

Hyacinth looked at Wiggs in despair.

"There!" she said. "That's me. I don't know what it is about the woman, but I feel just a child in front of her. Oh, Wiggs, Wiggs, I feel so lonely sometimes with nothing but women all around me. I wish I had a man here to help me."

"Are *all* the men fighting in *all* the countries?"

"Not all the countries. There's—Araby. Don't you remember—oh, but of course, you wouldn't know anything about it. But Father was just going to ask Prince Udo of Araby to come here on a visit when the war broke out. Oh, I wish, I *wish* Father were back again." She laid her head on her arms; and whether she would have shed a few royal tears or had a good homely cry, I cannot tell you. For at that moment an attendant came in. Hyacinth was herself again at once.

"There is a messenger approaching on a horse, your Royal Highness," she announced. "Doubtless from his Majesty's camp."

With a shriek of delight and an entire lack of royal dignity, the Princess, followed by the faithful Wiggs, rushed down to receive him.

Meanwhile, what of the Countess? She was still in the Palace, and, more than that, she was in the Throne Room of the Palace, and, more even than that, she was on the Throne of the Throne Room of the Palace.

She couldn't resist it. The door was open as she came down from her interview with the Princess, and she had to go in. There was a woman in there, tidying up, who looked questioningly at Belvane as she entered.

"You may leave," said the Countess, with dignity. "Her Royal Highness sent me in here to wait for her."

The woman curtsied and withdrew.

The Countess then uttered these extraordinary words:

"When I am Queen in Euralia, they shall leave me backward!"

Her subsequent behaviour was even more amazing.

She stood by the side of the door, and putting her hand to her mouth, said shrilly, "*Terrum, ter-rum, ter-rumty-umty-um*." Then she took her hand away and announced loudly, "Her Majesty Queen Belvane the First!" after which she cheered slightly.

Then in came her Majesty, a very proper, dignified, gracious Queen—none of your seventeen-year-old chits. Bowing condescendingly from side to side, she made her way to the Throne, and with a sweep of her train she sat down.

Courtiers were presented to her; representatives from foreign countries; Prince Hanspatch of Tregong, Prince Ulric, the Duke of Highanlow.

"Ah, my dear Prince Hanspatch," she cried, stretching out her hand to the right of her; "and you, dear Prince Ulric," with a graceful movement of the left arm toward him; "and, dear Duke, *you* also!" Her right hand, which Prince Hanspatch had by now finished with, went out to the Duke of Highanlow that he, too, might kiss it.

But it was arrested in mid-air. She felt rather than saw that the Princess was watching her in amazement from the doorway.

Without looking round, she stretched out again first one arm and then the other. Then, as if she had just seen the Princess, she jumped up in a pretty confusion.

"Oh, your Royal Highness," she cried, "you caught me at my physical exercises!" She gave a self-conscious little laugh. "My physical exercises—a forearm movement." Once again she stretched out her arm. "Building up the—er—building up—building up . . ."

Her voice died away, for the Princess still looked coldly at her.

"Charming, Countess," she said. "I am sorry to interrupt you, but I have some news for you. You will like to know that I am inviting Prince Udo of Araby here on a visit. I feel we want a little outside help in our affairs."

"Prince Udo?" cried the Countess. "*Here*?"

"Have you any objection?" said Hyacinth. She found it easier to be stern now, for the invitation had already been sent off by the hand of the King's messenger. Nothing that the Countess could say could influence her.

"No objection, your Royal Highness; but it seems so strange. And then the expense! Men are such hearty eaters. Besides"—she looked with a charming smile from the Princess to Wiggs—"we are all getting on so *nicely* together! Of course if he just dropped in for afternoon tea one day—"

"He will make a stay of some months, I hope." There were no wizards in Barodia, and therefore the war would be a long one. It was this which had decided Hyacinth.

"Of course," said Belvane, "whatever your Royal Highness wishes, but I do think that his Majesty—"

"My dear Countess," said Hyacinth, with a smile, "the invitation has already gone, so there's nothing more to be said, is there? Had you finished your exercises? Yes? Then, Wiggs, will you conduct her ladyship downstairs?"

She turned and left her. The Countess watched her go, and then stood tragically in the middle of the room, clasping her diary to her breast.

"This is terrible!" she said. "I feel *years* older." She held out her diary at arm's length and said in a gloomy voice, "*What* an entry for tomorrow!" The thought cheered her up a little. She began to consider plans. How could she circumvent this terrible young man who was going to put them all in their places? She wished that . . .

All at once she remembered something.

"Wiggs," she said, "what was it I heard you saying to the Princess about a wish?"

"Oh, that's my ring," said Wiggs eagerly. "If you've been good for a whole day you can have a good wish. And my wish is that—"

"A wish!" said Belvane to herself. "Well, I wish that . . ." A sudden thought struck her. "You said that you had to be *good* for a whole day first?"

"Yes."

Belvane mused.

"I wonder what they mean by *good*," she said.

"Of course," explained Wiggs, "if you've been bad for a whole day, you can have a bad wish. But I should hate to have a bad wish, wouldn't you?"

"Simply hate it, child," said Belvane. "Er—may I have a look at that ring?"

"Here it is," said Wiggs; "I always wear it round my neck."

The Countess took it from her.

"Listen," she said. "Wasn't that the Princess calling you? Run along, quickly, child." She almost pushed her from the room and closed the door on her.

Alone again, she paced from end to end of the great chamber, her left hand nursing her right elbow, her chin in her right hand.

"If you are good for a day," she mused, "you can have a good wish. If you are bad for a day, you can have a bad wish. Yesterday I drew ten thousand pieces of gold for the Army; the actual expenses were what I paid—what I owe Woggs. . . . I suppose that is what narrow-minded people call being bad. . . . I suppose this Prince Udo would call it bad. . . . I suppose he thinks he will marry the Princess and throw me into prison." She flung her head back proudly. "Never!"

Standing in the middle of the great Throne Room, she held the ring up in her two hands and wished.

"I wish," she said, and there was a terrible smile in her eyes, "I wish that something very—very *humorous* shall happen to Prince Udo on his journey."

8
Prince Udo Sleeps Badly

EVERYBODY LIKES TO make a good impression on his first visit, but there were moments just before his arrival in Euralia when Prince Udo doubted whether the affair would go as well as he had hoped. You shall hear why.

He had been out hunting with his friend, the young Duke Coronel, and was returning to the Palace when Hyacinth's messenger met him. He took the letter from him, broke the seals, and unrolled it.

"Wait a moment, Coronel," he said to his friend. "This is going to be an adventure of some sort, and if it's an adventure, I shall want you with me."

"I'm in no hurry," said Coronel, and he got off his horse and gave it into the care of an attendant. The road crossed a stream here. Coronel sat up on the little stone bridge and dropped pebbles idly into the water.

The Prince read his letter.

Plop . . . plop . . . plop . . . plop . . .

The Prince looked up from his letter.

"How many days' journey is it to Euralia?" he asked Coronel.

"How long did it take the messenger to come?" answered Coronel, without looking up. *(Plop.)*

"I might have thought of that myself," said Udo, "only this letter has rather upset me." He turned to the messenger. "How long has it—"

"Isn't the letter dated?" said Coronel. *(Plop.)*

Udo paid no attention to this interruption and finished his question to the messenger.

"A week, sire."

"Ride on to the castle and wait for me. I shall have a message for you."

"What is it?" said Coronel, when the messenger had gone. "An adventure?"

"I think so. I think we may call it that, Coronel."

"With me in it?"

"Yes, I think you will be somewhere in it."

Coronel stopped dropping his pebbles and turned to the Prince.

"May I hear about it?"

Udo held out the letter; then, feeling that a lady's letter should be private, drew it back again. He prided himself always on doing the correct thing.

"It's from Princess Hyacinth of Euralia," he

said; "she doesn't say much. Her father is away fighting, and she is alone and she is in some trouble or other. It ought to make rather a good adventure."

Coronel turned away and began to drop his pebbles into the stream again.

"Well, I wish you luck," he said. "If it's a dragon, don't forget that—"

"But you're coming, too," said Udo, in dismay. "I must have you with me."

"Doing what?"

"What?"

"Doing what?" said Coronel again.

"Well," said Prince Udo awkwardly, "er—well, you—well."

He felt that it was a silly question for Coronel to have asked. Coronel knew perfectly well what he would be doing all the time. In Udo's absence he would be telling Princess Hyacinth stories of his Royal Highness's matchless courage and wisdom. An occasional discussion also with the Princess upon types of masculine beauty, leading up to casual mention of Prince Udo's own appearance, would be quite in order. When Prince Udo was present Coronel would no doubt find the opportunity of drawing Prince Udo out, an opportunity of which a stranger could not so readily avail himself.

But of course you couldn't very well tell Coronel that. A man of any tact would have seen it at once.

"Of course," he said, "don't come if you don't like. But it would look rather funny if I went quite unattended; and—and her Royal Highness is said to be very beautiful," he added lamely.

Coronel laughed. There are adventures and adventures; to sit next to a very beautiful Princess and discuss with her the good looks of another man was not the sort of adventure that Coronel was looking for.

He tossed the remainder of his pebbles into the stream and stood up.

"Of course, if your Royal Highness wishes—"

"Don't be a fool, Coronel," said his Royal Highness rather snappily.

"Well, then, I'll come with my good friend Udo if he wants me."

"I do want you."

"Very well, that settles it. After all," he added to himself, "there may be *two* dragons."

Two dragons would be one each. But from all accounts there were not two Princesses.

So three days later the friends set out with good hearts upon the adventure. The messenger had been sent back to announce their arrival; they gave him three days' start, and hoped to gain two days upon him. In the simple fashion of those times (so it would seem from Roger Scurvilegs), they set out with no luggage and no clear idea of where they were going to sleep at night. This, after all, is the best spirit in which to start a journey. It is the Gladstone bag which has killed romance.

They started on a perfect summer day, and they rode past towers and battlements, and by the side of sparkling streams, and disappeared into tall pine forests, and came out into the sunlight again above sleepy villages, and, as they rode, Coronel sang aloud and Udo tossed his sword into the air and caught it again. And as evening fell they came to a woodman's cottage at the foot of a high hill, and there they decided to rest for the night. An old woman came out to welcome them.

"Good evening, your Royal Highness," she said.

"You know me?" said Udo, more pleased than surprised.

"I know all who come into my house," said the old woman solemnly, "and all who go away from it."

This sort of conversation made Coronel feel creepy. There seemed to be a distinction between the people who came into the house and the people who went away from it which he did not like.

"Can we stay here the night, my good woman?" said Udo.

"You have hurt your hand," she said, taking no notice of his question.

"It's nothing," said Udo hastily. On one occasion he had caught his sword by the sharp end by mistake—a foolish thing to have done.

"Ah, well, since you won't want hands where you're going, it won't matter much."

It was the sort of thing old women said in those days, and Udo did not pay much attention to it.

"Yes, yes," he said; "but can you give my friend and myself a bed for tonight?"

"Seeing that you won't be traveling together long, come in and welcome."

She opened the door and they followed her in.

As they crossed the threshold, Udo half turned round and whispered over his shoulder to Coronel.

"Probably a Fairy. Be kind to her."

"How can one be kind to one's hostess?" said Coronel. "It's she who has to be kind to *us*."

"Well, you know what I mean; don't be rude to her."

"My dear Udo, this to *me*—the pride of Araby, the favourite courtier of his Majesty, the—"

"Oh, all right," said Udo.

"Sit down and rest yourselves," said the old woman. "There'll be something in the pot for you directly."

"Good," said Udo. He looked approvingly at the large cauldron hanging over the fire. It was a big fireplace for such a small room. So he thought when he first looked at it, but as he gazed, the room seemed to get bigger and bigger, and the fireplace to get farther and farther away, until he felt that he was in a vast cavern cut deep into the mountainside. He rubbed his eyes, and there he was in the small kitchen again and the cauldron was sending out a savoury smell.

"There'll be something in it for all tastes," went on the old woman, "even for Prince Udo's."

"I'm not so particular as all that," said Udo mildly. The room had just become five hundred yards long again, and he was feeling quiet.

"Not now, but you will be."

She filled them a plate each from the pot; and pulling their chairs up to the table, they fell to heartily.

"This is really excellent," said Udo as he put down his spoon and rested for a moment.

"You'd think you'd always like that, wouldn't you?" she said.

"I always shall be fond of anything so perfectly cooked."

"Ah," remarked the old woman thoughtfully.

Udo was beginning to dislike her particular style of conversation. It seemed to carry the merest suggestion of a hint that something unpleasant might be going to happen to him. Nothing apparently was going to happen to Coronel.

He tried to drag Coronel into the conversation in case the old woman had anything over him.

"My friend and I," he said, "hope to be in Euralia the day after tomorrow."

"No harm in hoping," was the answer.

"Dear me, is something going to happen to us on the way?"

"Depends what you call 'us.' "

Coronel pushed back his chair and got up.

"I know what's going to happen to me," he said. "I'm going to sleep."

"Well," said Udo, getting up, too, "we've got a long day before us tomorrow, and apparently we are in for an adventure—er, *we* are in for an adventure of some sort." He looked anxiously at the old woman, but she made no sign. "And so let's to bed."

"This way," said the old woman, and by the light of a candle she led them upstairs.

Udo slept badly. He had a feeling (just as you have) that something was going to happen to him; and it was with some surprise that he woke up in the morning to find himself much as he was when he went to bed. He looked at himself in the glass; he invited Coronel to gaze at him; but neither could discover that anything was the matter.

"After all," said Udo, "I don't suppose she meant anything. These old women get into a way of talking like that. If anybody is going to be turned into anything, it's much more likely to be you."

"Is that why you brought me with you?" asked Coronel.

I suppose that by this time they had finished their dressing. Roger Scurvilegs tells us nothing on such important matters; no doubt from modesty. "Next morning they rose," he says, and disappoints us of a picture of Udo brushing his hair. They rose and went down to breakfast.

The old woman was in a less cryptic mood at breakfast. She was particularly hospitable to Udo, and from some secret store produced an unending variety of good things for him to eat. To Coronel it almost looked as if she were fattening him up for something, but this suggestion was received with such bad grace by Udo that he did not pursue the subject.

As soon as breakfast was over, they started off again. From one of the many bags of gold he carried, Udo had offered some acknowledgment to the old woman, but she had refused to take it.

"Nay, nay," she said. "I shall be amply rewarded before the day is out." And she seemed to be smiling to herself, as if she knew of some joke which the Prince and Coronel did not yet share.

"I like today," said Coronel as they rode along.

"There's a smell of adventure in the air. Red roofs, green trees, blue sky, white road—I could fall in love today."

"Who with?" said Udo suspiciously.

"Anyone—that old woman, if you like."

"Oh, don't talk of her," said the Prince, with a shudder. "Coronel, hadn't you a sense of being *out* of some joke that she was in?"

"Perhaps we shall be in it before long. I could laugh very easily on a morning like this."

"Oh, I can see a joke as well as anyone," said Udo. "Don't be afraid that I shan't laugh, too. No doubt it will make a good story, whatever it is, to tell to the Princess Hyacinth. Coronel," he added solemnly, the thought having evidently only just occurred to him, "I am all impatience to help that poor girl in her trouble." And as if to show his impatience, he suddenly gave the reins a shake and cantered ahead of his companion. Smiling to himself, Coronel followed at his leisure.

They halted at midday in a wood, and made a meal from some provisions which the old woman had given them; and after they had eaten, Udo lay down on a mossy bank and closed his eyes.

"I'm sleepy," he said; "I had a restless night. Let's stay here awhile; after all, there's no hurry."

"Personally," said Coronel, "I'm all impatience to help that—"

"I told you I had a very bad night," said Udo crossly.

"Oh, well, I shall go off and look for dragons. Coronel, the Dragon Slayer. Goodbye."

"Only half an hour," said Udo.

"Right."

With a nod to the Prince, he strolled off among the trees.

9
They Are Afraid of Udo

THIS IS A painful chapter for me to write. Mercifully, it is to be a short one. Later on I shall become used to the situation; inclined, even, to dwell upon its humorous side; but for the moment I cannot see beyond the sadness of it. That to a Prince of the Royal House of Araby, and such an estimable young man as Udo, those things should happen. Roger Scurvilegs frankly breaks down over it. "That abominable woman," he says (meaning, of course, Belvane), and he has hysterics for more than a page.

Let us describe it calmly.

Coronel came back from his stroll in the same casual way in which he had started, and dropped down lazily upon the grass to wait until Udo was ready to mount. He was not thinking of Udo. He was wondering if Princess Hyacinth had an attendant of surpassing beauty, or a dragon of surpassing malevolence—if, in fact, there were any adventures in Euralia for a humble fellow like himself.

"Coronel!" said a small voice behind him.

He turned around indifferently.

"Hullo, Udo, where are you?" he said. "Isn't it time we were starting?"

"We aren't starting," said the voice.

"What's the matter? What are you hiding in the bushes for? Whatever's the matter, Udo?"

"I'm not very well."

"My poor Udo, what's happened?" He jumped up and made toward him.

"Stop!" shrieked the voice. "I command you!"

Coronel stopped.

"Your Royal Highness's commands . . ." he began rather coldly.

There was an ominous sniffing from the bushes.

"Coronel," said an unhappy voice at last, "I think I'm coming out."

Wondering what it all meant, Coronel waited in silence.

"Yes, I am coming out, Coronel," said the voice. "But you mustn't be surprised if I don't look very well. I'm—I'm—Coronel, here I am," said Udo pathetically, and he stepped out.

Coronel didn't know whether to laugh or to cry.

Poor Prince Udo!

He had the head and the long ears of a rabbit, and in some unfortunate way a look of the real Prince Udo in spite of it. He had the mane and the tail of a lion. In between the tail and the mane it is difficult to say what he was, save that there was an impression of magnificence about his person—such magnificence, anyhow, as is given by an astrakhan-trimmed fur coat.

Coronel decided that it was an occasion for tact.

"Ah, here you are," he said cheerfully. "Shall we get along?"

"Don't be a fool, Coronel," said Udo, almost crying. "Don't pretend that you can't *see* that I've got a tail."

"Why, bless my soul, so you have. A tail! Well, think of that!"

Udo showed what he thought of it by waving it peevishly.

"This is not a time for tact," he said. "Tell me what I look like."

Coronel considered for a moment.

"Really frankly?" he asked.

"Y—yes," said Udo nervously.

"Then, frankly, your Royal Highness looks—funny."

"*Very* funny?" said Udo wistfully.

"*Very* funny," said Coronel.

His Highness sighed.

"I was afraid so," he said. "That's the cruel

part about it. Had I been a lion, there would have been a certain pathetic splendour about my position. Isolated—cut off—suffering in regal silence." He waved an explanatory paw. "Even in the most hideous of beasts there might be a dignity." He meditated for a moment. "Have you ever seen a yak, Coronel?" he asked.

"Never."

"I saw one once in Barodia. It is not a beautiful animal, Coronel; but as a yak I should not have been entirely unlovable. One does not laugh at a yak, Coronel, and where one does not laugh, one may come to love. . . . What does my head look like?"

"It looks—striking."

"I haven't seen it, you see."

"To one who didn't know your Royal Highness it would convey the impression of a rabbit."

Udo laid his head between his paws and wept.

"A r—rabbit!" he sobbed. "So undignified, so lacking in true pathos, so . . . And not even a whole rabbit," he added bitterly.

"How did it happen?"

"I don't know, Coronel. I just went to sleep, and woke up feeling rather funny, and . . ." He sat up suddenly and stared at Coronel. "It was that old woman who did it. You mark my words, Coronel; she did it."

"Why should she?"

"I don't know. I was very polite to her. Don't

you remember my saying to you, 'Be polite to her, because she's probably a Fairy!' You see, I saw through her disguise at once. Coronel, what shall we do? Let's hold a council of war and think it over."

So they held a council of war.

Prince Udo put forward two suggestions.

The first was that Coronel should go back on the morrow and kill the old woman.

The second was that Coronel should go back that afternoon and kill the old woman.

Coronel pointed out that as she turned Prince Udo into—into a—a—("Quite so," said Udo)—it was likely that she alone could turn him back again, and that in that case he had better only threaten her.

"I want *somebody* killed," said Udo, rather naturally.

"Suppose," said Coronel, "you stay here for two days while I go back and see the old witch, and make her tell me what she knows. She knows something, I'm certain. Then we shall see better what to do."

Udo mused for a space.

"Why didn't they turn *you* into anything?" he asked.

"Really, I don't know. Perhaps because I'm too unimportant."

"Yes, that must be it." He began to feel a little brighter. "Obviously, that's it." He caressed a whisker with one of his paws. "They were afraid of me."

He began to look so much happier that Coronel thought it was a favourable moment in which to withdraw.

"Shall I go now, your Royal Higness?"

"Yes, yes, you may leave me."

"And shall I find you here when I come back?"

"You may or may not, Coronel; you may or you may not. . . . Afraid of me," he murmured to himself. "Obviously."

"And if I don't?"

"Then return to the Palace."

"Goodbye, your Royal Highness."

Udo waved a paw at him.

"Goodbye, goodbye."

Coronel got on his horse and rode away. As soon as he was out of earshot, he began to laugh. Spasm after spasm shook him. No sooner had he composed himself to gravity than a remembrance of Udo's appearance started him off again.

I couldn't have stayed with him a moment longer, he thought. I should have burst. Poor Udo! However, we'll soon get him all right.

That evening he reached the place where the cottage had stood, but it was gone. Next morning he rode back to the wood. Udo was gone, too. He returned to the Palace, and began to think it out.

*   *   *

Left to himself, Udo very soon made up his mind. There were three courses open to him.

He might stay where he was till he was restored to health.

This he rejected at once. When you have the head of a rabbit, the tail of a lion, and the middle of a woolly lamb, the need for action of some kind is imperative. All the blood of your diverse ancestors calls to you to be up and doing.

He might go back to Araby.

To Araby, where he was so well known, so respected, so popular? To Araby, where he rode daily among his father's subjects, that they might have the pleasure of cheering him? How awkward for everybody!

On to Euralia then?

Why not? The Princess Hyacinth had called for him. What devotion it showed if he came to her even now—in his present state of bad health! She was in trouble: enchanters, wizards, whatnots. Already, then, he had suffered in her service—so, at least, he would say, and so, possibly, it might be. Coronel had thought him—funny; but women had not much sense of humour as a rule. Probably as a child Hyacinth had kept rabbits . . . or lambs. She would find him—strokable. . . . And the lion in him . . . in his tail, his fierce mane . . . she would find that inspiring. Women like to feel that there is something fierce, untamable in the man they love; well, there it was.

It was not as if he had Coronel with him. Coronel and he (in his present health) could never have gone into Euralia together; the contrast was too striking; but he alone, Hyacinth's only help! Surely she would appreciate his magnanimity.

Also, as he had told himself a moment ago, there was quite a chance that it was a Euralian enchanter who had put this upon him—to prevent him helping Hyacinth. If so, he had better go to Euralia in order to deal with that enchanter. For the moment, he did not see exactly how to deal with him, but no doubt he would think of some tremendously cunning device later on.

To Euralia then with all dispatch.

He trotted off. As Coronel had said, they were evidently afraid of him.

10
Charlotte Patacake Astonishes the Critics

THE LADY BELVANE sits in her garden. She is very happy. An enormous quill pen, taken from a former favourite goose and coloured red, is in her right hand. The hair of her dark head, held on one side, touches the paper whereon she writes, and her little tongue peeps out between her red lips. Her left hand taps the table—one-two, one-two, one-two, one-two, one-two. She is composing.

Wonderful woman!

You remember that scene with Princess Hyacinth? "I feel we want a little outside help in our affairs." A fortnight of suspense before Prince Udo arrived. What had the ring done to him? At the best, even if there would be no Udo at all to interfere, nevertheless she knew that she had lost her footing at the Palace. She and the Princess would now be open enemies. At the

worst—those magic rings were so untrustworthy!
—a Prince, still powerful, and now seriously
annoyed, might be leagued against her.

Yet she composed.

And what is she writing? She is entering for
the competition in connection with the Encouragement of Literature Scheme: the last scheme
which the Princess had signed.

I like to think of her peacefully writing at a
time when her whole future hung in the bal-
ance. Roger sneers at her. "Even now," he says,
"she was hoping to wring a last bagful of gold
from her wretched country." I deny emphati-
cally that she was doing anything of the sort.
She was entering for a duly authorized competition under the pen name of Charlotte Patacake.
The fact that the Countess Belvane, according
to the provisions of the scheme, was sole judge
of the competition is beside the point. Belvane's
opinion of Charlotte Patacake's poetry was utterly
sincere, and uninfluenced in any way by mone-
tary considerations. If Patacake were awarded
the first prize, it would be because Belvane hon-
estly thought she was worth it.

One other fact by way of defence against
Roger's slanders. As judge, Belvane had chosen
the subject of the prize poems. Now Belvane
and Patacake both excelled in the lighter forms
of lyrical verse; yet the subject of the poem was
to be epic. "The Barodo-Euralian War"—no less.
How many modern writers would be as fair?

THE BARODO-EURALIAN WAR

This line is written in gold, and by itself would obtain a prize in any local competition.

> "King Merriwig the First rode out to war
> As many other kings had done before!
> Five hundred men behind him marched to
>   fight—"

There follows a good deal of scratching out, and then comes (a sudden inspiration) this sublimely simple line:

> "Left-right, left-right, left-right, left-right,
>   left-right."

One can almost hear the men moving.

> "What gladsome cheers assailed the balmy air—
> They came from north, from south, from every-
>   where!
> No wight that stood upon that sacred scene
> Could gaze upon the sight unmoved, I ween:
> No wight that stood upon that sacred spot
> Could gaze upon the sight unmoved, I wot:"

It is not quite clear whether the last couplet is an alternative to the couplet before or is purposely added in order to straighten it. Looking over her left shoulder, it seems to me that there is a line drawn through the first one, but I cannot see very clearly because of her hair, which will keep straying over the page.

"Why do they march so fearless and so bold?
The answer is not very quickly told.
To put it shortly, the Barodian king
Insulted Merriwig like anything—
King Merriwig, the dignified and wise,
Who saw him flying over with surprise,
As did his daughter, Princess Hyacinth."

This was as far as she had got.

She left the table and began to walk round her garden. There is nothing like it for assisting thought. However, today it was not helping much; she went three times round and still couldn't think of a rhyme for Hyacinth. *Plinth* was a little difficult to work in; "Besides," she reminded herself, "I don't quite know what it means." Belvane felt as I do about poetry: that however incomprehensible it may be to the public, the author should be quite at ease with it.

She added up the lines she had written already—seventeen. If she stopped there, it would be the only epic that had stopped at the seventeenth line.

She sighed, stretched her arms, and looked up at the sky. The weather was all against her. It was the ideal largesse morning. . . .

Twenty minutes later she was on her cream-white palfrey. Twenty-one minutes later Henrietta Crossbuns had received a bag of gold neatly under the eye, as she bobbed to her Ladyship. To this extent only did H. Crossbuns leave her mark upon Euralia history; but it was a mark which lasted for a full month.

Hyacinth knew nothing of all this. She did not even know that Belvane was entering for the prize poem. She had forgotten her promise to encourage literature in the realm.

And why? Ah, ladies, can you not guess why? She was thinking of Prince Udo of Araby. What did he look like? Was he dark or fair? Did his hair curl naturally or not?

Was he wondering at all what *she* looked like?

Wiggs had already decided that he was to fall in love with her Royal Highness and marry her.

"I think," said Wiggs, "that he'll be very tall, and have lovely blue eyes and golden hair."

This was what they were like in all the books she had ever dusted; like this were the seven Princes (now pursuing perilous adventures in distant countries) to whom the King had promised Hyacinth's hand—Prince Hanspatch of Tregong, Prince Ulric, the Duke of Highanlow, and all the rest of them. Poor Price Ulric! In the moment of victory he was accidentally fallen upon by the giant whom he was engaged in undermining, and lost all appetite for adventure thereby. Indeed, in his latter years he was alarmed by anything larger than a goldfish, and lived a life of the strictest seclusion.

"*I* think he'll be dark," said Hyacinth. Her own hair was corn-coloured.

Poor Prince Hanspatch of Tregong; I've just remembered about him—no, I haven't, it was the Duke of Highanlow. Poor Duke of Highanlow! A misunderstanding with a wizard having caused his head to face the wrong way round, he was so often said goodbye to at the very moment of arrival that he gradually lost his enthusiasm for social enterprises and confined himself to his own palace, where his acrobatic dexterity in supplying himself with soup was a constant source of admiration to his servants. . . .

However, it was Prince Udo of whom they were thinking now. The messenger had returned from Araby; his Royal Highness must be expected on the morrow.

"I do hope he'll be comfortable in the Purple Room," said Hyacinth. "I wonder if it wouldn't have been better to have left him in the Blue Room, after all."

They had had him in the Blue Room two days ago, until Hyacinth thought that perhaps he would be more comfortable in the Purple Room, after all.

"The Purple Room has the best view," said Wiggs helpfully.

"And it gets the sun. Wiggs, don't forget to put some flowers there. And have you given him any books?"

"I gave him two," said Wiggs. "*Quests for Princes*, and *Wild Animals at Home*."

"Oh, I'm sure he'll like those. Now let's think what we shall do when he comes. He'll arrive some time in the afternoon. Naturally he will want a little refreshment."

"Would he like a picnic in the forest?" asked Wiggs.

"I don't think anyone wants a picnic after a long journey."

"I *love* picnics."

"Yes, dear; but, you see, Prince Udo's much older than you, and I expect he's had so many picnics that he's tired of them. I suppose really I ought to receive him in the Throne Room, but that's so—so—"

"Stuffy," said Wiggs.

"That's just it. We should feel uncomfortable with each other the whole time. I think I shall receive him up here; I never feel so nervous in the open air."

"Will the Countess be here?" asked Wiggs.

"No," said the Princess coldly. "At least," she corrected herself, "she will not be invited. Good afternoon, Countess." It was like her, thought Hyacinth, to arrive at that very moment.

Belvane curtsied low.

"Good afternoon, your Royal Highness. I am here purely on a matter of business. I thought it my duty to inform your Royal Highness of the result of the Literature prize." She spoke meekly, and as one who forgave Hyacinth for her unkindess toward her.

"Certainly, Countess. I shall be glad to hear."

The Countess unrolled a parchment.

"The prize has been won," she said, "by" —she held the parchment a little closer to her eyes—"by Charlotte Patacake."

"Oh, yes. Who is she?"

"A most deserving woman, your Royal Highness. If she is the woman I'm thinking of, a most deserving person, to whom the money will be more than welcome. Her poem shows a sense of values combined with—er—breadth, and—er—distance, such as I have seldom seen equalled. The—er—technique is only excelled by the—shall I say?—temperamentality, the boldness of the colouring, by the—how shall I put it?—the firmness of the outline. In short—"

"In short," said the Princess, "you like it."

"Your Royal Highness, it is unique. But naturally you will wish to hear it for yourself. It is only some twelve hundred lines long. I will declaim it to your Royal Highness."

She held the manuscript out at the full length of her left arm, struck an attitude with the right arm, and began in her most thrilling voice:

" 'King Merriwig the First rode out to war,
As many other kings—' "

"Yes, Countess, but another time. I am busy this afternoon. As you know, I think, the Prince Udo of Araby arrives tomorrow, and . . ."

Belvane's lips were still moving, and her right arm swayed up and down. " 'What gladsome cheers assailed the balmy air!' " she murmured to herself, and her hand went up to heaven. " 'They come from north, from south' " (she pointed in the directions mentioned), " 'from everywhere. No wight that stood— ' "

"He will be received privately up here by myself in the first place, and afterwards—"

" 'Could gaze upon the sight unmoved, I wot,' " whispered Belvane, and placed her hand upon her breast to show that anyhow it had been too much for *her*. " 'Why do they march so . . .' I beg your Royal Highness's pardon. I was so carried away by this wonderful poem. I do beg of your Royal Highness to read it."

The Princess waved the manuscript aside.

"I am not unmindful of the claims of literature, Countess, and I shall certainly read the poem another time. Meanwhile I can, I hope, trust you to see that the prize is awarded to the rightful winner. What I am telling you now is that the Prince Udo is arriving tomorrow."

Belvane looked innocently puzzled.

"Prince Udo—Udo—would that be Prince Udo of Carroway, your Royal Highness? A tall man with three legs?"

"Prince Udo of Araby," said Hyacinth severely. "I think I have already mentioned him to your ladyship. He will make a stay of some months."

"But how *delightful*, your Royal Highness, to see a man again! We were all getting so dull together! We want a man to wake us up a little, don't we, Wiggs? I will go and give orders about his room at once, your Royal Highness. You will wish him to be in the Purple Room, of course?"

That settled it.

"He will be in the Blue Room," said Hyacinth decidedly.

"Certainly, your Royal Highess. Fancy, Wiggs, a man again! I will go and see about it now, if I may have your Royal Highness's leave to withdraw?"

A little mystified by Belvane's manner, Hyacinth inclined her head, and the Countess withdrew.

11

Water Cress Seems to Go With the Ears

WIGGS GAVE A parting pat to the tablecloth and stood looking at it with her head on one side.

"Now, then," she said, "have we got everything?"

"What about sardines?" said Woggs in her common way. (I don't know what she's doing in this scene at all, but Roger Scurvilegs insists on it.)

"I don't think a *Prince* would like *sardines*," said Wiggs.

"If *I'd* been on a long journey, I'd *love* sardines. It *is* a very long journey from Araby, isn't it?"

"Awfully long. Why, it's taken him nearly a week. Perhaps," she added hopefully, "he's had something on the way."

"Perhaps he took some sandwiches with him,"

said Woggs, thinking that this would be a good thing to do.

"What do you think he'll be like, Woggs?"

Woggs thought for a long time.

"Like the King," she said. "Only different," she added as an afterthought.

Up came the Princess for the fifth time that afternoon, all excitement.

"Well," she said, "is everything ready?"

"Yes, your Royal Highness. Except Woggs and me didn't quite know about sardines."

The Princess laughed happily.

"I think there will be enough for him. It all looks very nice."

She turned round, and discovered behind her the last person she wanted to see just then.

The-last-person-she-wanted-to-see-just-then curt-sied effectively.

"Forgive me, your Royal Highness," she said profusely, "but I thought I had left Charlotte Patacake's priceless manuscript up here. No; evidently I was mistaken, your Royal Highness. I will withdraw, your Royal Highness, as I know your Royal Highness would naturally wish to receive his Royal Highness alone."

Listening to this speech, one is impressed with Wogg's method of calling everybody "Mum."

"Not at all, Countess," said Hyacinth coldly. "We would prefer you to stay and help us receive his Royal Highness. He is a little late, I think."

Belvane looked unspeakably distressed.

"Oh, I do *hope* that nothing has happened to him on the way," she exclaimed. "I've had an uneasy feeling lately that something may have occurred."

"What could have happened to him?" asked Hyacinth, not apparently very much alarmed.

"Oh, your Royal Highness, it's just a sort of silly feeling of mine. There may be nothing in it."

There was a noise of footsteps from below; a man's voice was heard. The Princess and the Countess, both extremely nervous, but from entirely different reasons, arranged suitable smiles of greeting upon their faces; Wiggs and Woggs stood in attitudes of appropriate meekness by the table. The Court Painter could have made a beautiful picture of it.

"His Royal Highness Prince Udo of Araby," announced the voice of an attendant.

A nervous moment, said Belvane to herself. Can the ring have failed to act?

Udo trotted in.

"It hasn't," said Belvane.

Princess Hyacinth gave a shriek, and faltered slowly backward; Wiggs, who was familiar with these little accidents in the books which she dusted, and Woggs, who had a natural love for any kind of animal, stood their ground.

"Whatever is it?" murmured Hyacinth.

It was as well that Belvane was there.

"Allow me to present to your Royal Highness," she said, stepping forward, "his Royal Highness Prince Udo of Araby."

"Prince *Udo*?" said Hyacinth, all unwilling to believe it.

"I'm afraid so," said Udo gloomily. He had thought over this meeting a good deal in the last two or three days, and he realized now that he had underestimated the difficulties of it.

Hyacinth remembered that she was a Princess and a woman.

"I'm delighted to welcome your Royal Highness to Euralia," she said. "Won't you sit down—I mean up—er, down." (How *did* rabbits sit? Or whatever he was?)

Udo decided to sit up.

"Thank you. You've no idea how difficult it is to talk on four legs to somebody higher up. It strains the neck so."

There was an awkward silence. Nobody quite knew what to say.

Except Belvane.

She turned to Udo with her most charming smile.

"Did you have a pleasant journey?" she asked sweetly.

"No," said Udo coldly.

"Oh, do tell us what happened to you?" cried Hyacinth. "Did you meet some terrible enchanter on the way? Oh, I am so dreadfully sorry."

When one is not feeling very well, there is a certain type of question which is always annoying.

"Can't you *see* what's happened to me?" said Udo crossly. "I don't know *how* it happened. I had come two days' journey from Araby, when—"

"Please, your Royal Highness," said Wiggs, "is this *your* tail in the salt?" She took it out, gave it a shake, and handed it back to him.

"Oh, thank you, thank you—two days' journey from Araby when I woke up one afternoon and found myself like this. I ask you to imagine my annoyance. My first thought naturally was to return home and hide myself; but I told myself, Princess, that *you* wanted me."

The Princess could not help being touched by this, said as it was with a graceful movement of the ears and a caressing of the right whisker, but she wondered a little what she would do with him now that she had got him.

"Er—what *are* you?" put in Belvane kindly, knowing how men are always glad to talk about themselves.

Udo had caught sight of a well-covered table, and was looking at it with a curious mixture of hope and resignation.

"Very, very hungry," he said, speaking with the air of one who knows.

The Princess, whose mind had been travelling, woke up suddenly.

"Oh, I was forgetting my manners," she said, with a smile for which the greediest would have forgiven her. "Let us sit down and refresh ourselves. May I present to your Royal Highness the Countess Belvane."

"Do I shake hands or pat him?" murmured that mistress of Court etiquette, for once at a loss.

Udo placed a paw over his heart and bowed profoundly.

"Charmed," he said gallantly, and coming from a cross between a lion, a rabbit, and a woolly lamb, the merest suggestion of gallantry has a most pleasing effect.

They grouped themselves round the repast.

"A little sherbet, your Royal Highness?" said Hyacinth, who presided over the bowl.

Udo was evidently longing to say Yes, but hesitated.

"I wonder if I dare."

"It's very good sherbet," said Wiggs, to encourage him.

"I'm sure it is, my dear. But the question is, Do I like sherbet?"

"You can't help knowing if you like *sherbet*."

"Don't bother him, Wiggs," said Hyacinth, "a venison sandwich, dear Prince?"

"The question is, Do I like venison sandwiches?"

"*I* do," announced Woggs to anyone who was interested.

"You see," explained Udo, "I really don't know *what* I like."

They were all surprised at this, particularly Woggs. Belvane, who was enjoying herself too much to wish to do anything but listen, said nothing, and it was the Princess who obliged Udo by asking him what he meant. It was a subject upon which he was longing to let himself go to somebody.

"Well," he said, expanding himself a little, so that Wiggs had to remove his tail this time from the custard, "what am I?"

Nobody ventured to offer an opinion.

"Am I a hare? Then put me next to the red currant jelly, or whatever it is that hares like."

The anxious eye of the hostess wandered over the table.

"Am I a lion?" went on Udo, developing his theme. "Then pass me Wiggs."

"Oh, please don't be a lion," said Wiggs gently as she stroked his mane.

"But haven't you a feeling for anything?" asked Hyacinth.

"I have a great feeling of emptiness. I yearn for *something*, only I don't quite know what."

"I hope it isn't sardines," whispered Wiggs to Woggs.

"But what have you been eating on the way?" asked the Princess.

"Oh, grass and things chiefly. I thought I should be safe with grass."

"And were you—er—safe?" asked Belvane, with a great show of anxiety.

Udo coughed and said nothing.

"I know it's silly of me," said Hyacinth, "but I still don't quite understand. I should have thought that if you were a—a—"

"Quite so," said Udo.

". . . then you would have known by instinct what a—a—"

"Exactly," said Udo.

"Likes to eat."

"Ah, I thought you'd think that. That's just what I thought when this—when I began to feel unwell. But I've worked it out since, and it's all wrong."

"This *is* interesting," said Belvane, settling herself more comfortably. "*Do* go on."

"Well, when . . ." He coughed and looked around at them coyly. "This is really rather a delicate subject."

"Not at all," murmured Hyacinth.

"Well, it's like this. When an enchanter wants to annoy you, he generally turns you into an animal of some kind."

Belvane achieved her first blush since she was seventeen.

"It *is* a humorous way they have," she said.

"But suppose you really were an animal altogether, it wouldn't annoy you at all. An elephant isn't annoyed at being an elephant; he just tries to be a good elephant, and he'd be miserable if he couldn't do things with his trunk. The annoying thing is to look like an elephant, to have the very complicated—er—inside of an elephant, and yet all the time really to be a man."

They were all intensely interested. Woggs thought that it was going to lead up to a revelation of what sort of animal Prince Udo really was, but in this she was destined to be disappointed. After all, there were advantages in Udo's present position. As a man he had never been listened to so attentively.

"Now suppose for a moment I am a lion. I have the—er—delicate apparatus of a lion, but the beautiful thoughts and aspirations of a Prince. Thus there is one—er—side of me which craves for raw beef, but none the less there is a higher side of me" (he brought his paw up toward his heart), "which—well, you know how *you'd* feel about it yourself."

The Princess shuddered.

"I *should*," she said, with conviction.

Belvane was interested, but thought it all a little crude.

"You see the point," went on Udo. "A baby left to itself doesn't know what is good for it. Left to itself it would eat anything. Now turn a man suddenly into an animal, and he is in exactly the same state as that baby."

"I hadn't thought of it like that," said Hyacinth.

"I've *had* to think of it! Now let us proceed further with the matter." Udo was thoroughly enjoying himself. He had not had such a time since he had given an address on Beetles to all the leading citizens of Araby at his coming of age. "Suppose again that I am a lion. I know from what I have read or seen that raw meat agrees best with the lion's—er—organization, and however objectionable it might look, I should be foolish not to turn to it for sustenance. But if you don't quite know what animal you're supposed to be, see how difficult the problem becomes. It's a question of trying all sorts of horrible things in order to find out what agrees with you." His eyes took on a faraway look, a look in which the most poignant memories seemed to be reflected. "I've been experimenting," he said, "for the last three days."

They all gazed sadly and sympathetically at him. Except Belvane. She, of course, wouldn't.

"What went best?" she asked brightly.

"Oddly enough," said Udo, cheering up a little, "banana fritters. Have you ever kept an animal who lived entirely on banana fritters?"

"Never." The Princess smiled.

"Well, that's the animal I probably am." He

sighed and added, "There were one or two animals I wasn't." For a little while he seemed to be revolving bitter memories, and then went on, "I don't suppose any of you here have any idea how very prickly thistles are when they are going down. Er—may I try a water-cress sandwich? It doesn't suit the tail, but it seems to go with the ears." He took a large bite, and added through the leaves, "I hope I don't bore you, Princess, with my little troubles."

Hyacinth clasped his paw impulsively.

"My dear Prince Udo, I'm only longing to help. We must think of some way of getting this horrible enchantment off you. There are so many wise books in the library, and my father once composed a spell which—oh, I'm sure we shall soon have you all right again."

Udo took another sandwich.

"Very good of you, Princess, to say so. You understand how annoying a little indisposition of this kind is to a man of my temperament." He beckoned to Wiggs. "How do you make these?" he asked in an undertone.

Gracefully undulating, Belvane rose from her seat.

"Well," she said, "I must go and see that the . . . ." She broke off in a pretty confusion— "How silly of me, I mean, the Royal Apartment, prepared. Have I your Royal Highness's leave to withdraw?"

She had.

"And, Wiggs, dear, you, too, had better run along and see if you can help. You may leave the water-cress sandwiches," she added as Wiggs hesitated for a moment.

With a grateful look at her Royal Highness Udo helped himself to another one.

12
We Decide to Write
to Udo's Father

"NOW, MY DEAR Princess," said Udo, as soon as they were alone. "Let me know what way I can help you."

"Oh, Prince Udo," said Hyacinth earnestly, "it *is* good of you to have come. I feel that this—this little accident is really my fault for having asked you here."

"Not at all, dear lady. It is the sort of little accident that might have happened to anybody, anywhere. If I can still be of assistance to you, pray inform me. Though my physical powers may not for the moment be quite what they were, I flatter myself that my mental capabilities are in no way diminished." He took another bite of his sandwich and wagged his head wisely at her.

"Let's come over here," said Hyacinth.

She moved across to an old stone seat in the

wall, Udo following with the plate, and made room for him by her side. There is, of course, a way of indicating to a gentleman that he may sit next to you on the Chesterfield, and tell you what he has been doing in town lately, and there is also another way of patting the sofa for Fido to jump up and be-a-good-dog-and-lie-down-sir. Hyacinth achieved something very tactful in between, and Udo jumped up gracefully.

"Now we can talk," said Hyacinth. "You noticed that lady, the Countess Belvane, whom I presented to you?"

Udo nodded.

"What did you think of her?"

Udo was old enough to know what to say to that.

"I hardly looked at her," he said. And he added with a deep bow, "Naturally, when your Royal Highness—oh, I beg your pardon, are my ears in your way?"

"It's all right," said Hyacinth, rearranging her hair. "Well, it was because of that woman that I sent for you."

"But I can't marry her like this, your Royal Highness."

Hyacinth turned a startled face toward him. Udo perceived that he had blundered. To hide his confusion he took another sandwich and ate it very quickly.

"I want your help against her," said Hyacinth a little distantly; "she is plotting against me."

"Oh, your Royal Highness, now I see," said Udo, and he wagged his head as much as to say, "You've come to the right man this time."

"I don't trust her," said Hyacinth impressively.

"Well, now, Princess, I'm not surprised. I'll tell you something about that woman."

"Oh, what?"

"Well, when I was announced just now, what happened? You, yourself, Princess, were not unnaturally a little alarmed; those two little girls were surprised and excited; but what of this Countess Belvane? What did *she* do?"

"What *did* she do?"

"Nothing," said Udo impressively. "She was neither surprised nor alarmed."

"Why, now I come to think of it, I don't believe she was."

"And yet," said Udo half pathetically, half proudly, "Princes don't generally look like this. Now, why wasn't she surprised?"

Hyacinth looked bewildered.

"Did she know you were sending for me?" Udo went on.

"Yes."

"Because you had found out something about her?"

"Yes."

"Then depend upon it, *she's* done it. *What* a mind that woman must have!"

"But how could she do it?" exclaimed Hyacinth. "Of course it's just the sort of thing she *would* do if she could."

Udo didn't answer. He was feeling rather annoyed with Belvane, and had got off his seat and was trotting up and down so as not to show his feelings before a lady.

"How *could* she do it?" implored Hyacinth.

"Oh, she's in with some enchanter or somebody," said Udo impatiently as he trotted past.

Suddenly he had an idea. He stopped in front of her.

"If only I were *sure* I was a lion."

He tried to roar, exclaimed hastily that it was only a practice one, and roared again. "No, I don't think I'm a lion after all," he admitted sadly.

"Well," said Hyacinth, "we must think of a plan."

"We must think of a plan," said Udo, and he came and sat meekly beside her again. He could conceal it from himself no longer that he was not a lion. The fact depressed him.

"I suppose I have been weak," went on Hyacinth, "but ever since the men went away, she has been the ruling spirit of the country. I think she is plotting against me; I *know* she is robbing me. I asked you here so that you could help me to find her out."

Udo nodded his head importantly.

"We must watch her," he announced.

"We must watch her," agreed Hyacinth. "It may take months—"

"Did you say months?" said Udo, turning to her excitedly.

"Yes, why?"

"Well, it's . . ." He gave a deprecating little cough. "I know it's very silly of me but—oh, well, let's hope it will be all right."

"Why, whatever is the matter?"

Udo was decidedly embarrassed. He wriggled. He drew little circles with his hind paw on the ground and he shot little coy glances at her.

"Well, I"—and he gave a little nervous giggle—"I have a sort of uneasy feeling that I may be one of those animals"—he gave another conscious little laugh—"that have to go to sleep all through the winter. It would be very annoying —if I"—his paw became very busy here—"if I had to dig a little hole in the ground, just when the plot was thickening."

"Oh, but you won't," said Hyacinth, in distress.

They were both silent for a moment, thinking of the awful possibilities. Udo's tail had fallen across Hyacinth's lap, and she began to play with it absently.

"Anyway," she said hopefully, "it's only July now."

"Ye—es," said Udo. "I suppose I should get—er—busy about November. We ought to find out something before then. First of all we'd better . . . Oh!" He started up in dismay. "I've just had a *horrible* thought. Don't I have to collect a little store of nuts and things?"

"Surely—"

"I should have to start that pretty soon," said Udo thoughtfully. "You know, I shouldn't be very handy at it. Climbing about after nuts," he went on dreamily, "what a life for a—"

"Oh, don't!" pleaded Hyacinth. "Surely only squirrels do that?"

"Yes—yes. Now, if I were a squirrel, I should —may I have my tail for a moment?"

"Oh, I'm so sorry," said Hyacinth, very much confused as she realized the liberty she had been taking, and she handed his tail back to him.

"Not at all," said Udo.

He took it firmly in his right hand. "Now then," he said, "we shall see. Watch this."

Sitting up on his back legs, he arched his tail over his head, and letting go of it suddenly, began to nibble at a sandwich held in his two front paws . . . .

A pretty picture for an artist.

But a bad model. The tail fell with a thud to the ground.

"There!" said Udo triumphantly. "That proves it. I'm *not* a squirrel."

"Oh, I'm so glad," said Hyacinth, completely convinced, as anyone would have been, by this demonstration.

"Yes, well, that's all right then. Now we can make our plans. First of all, we'd better . . ." He stopped suddenly, and Hyacinth saw that he was gazing at his tail.

"Yes?" she said encouragingly.

He picked up his tail and held it out in front of him. There was a large knot in the middle of it.

"Now, *what* have I forgotten?" he said, rubbing his head thoughtfully.

Poor Hyacinth!

"Oh, dear Prince Udo, I'm so sorry. I'm afraid I did that without thinking."

Udo, the gallant gentleman, was not found wanting.

"A lover's knot," he said, with a graceful incli— No, he stopped in time. But really, those ears of his made ordinary politeness quite impossible.

"Oh, Udo," said Hyacinth impulsively, "if only I could help you to get back to your proper form again."

"Yes, if only," said Udo, becoming practical again; "but how are we going to do it? Just one more watercress sandwich," he said apologetically; "they go with the ears so well."

"I shall threaten the Countess," said Hyacinth excitedly. "I shall tell her that unless she makes the enchanter restore you to your proper form, I shall put her in prison."

Udo was not listening. He had gone off into his own thoughts. "Banana fritters *and* watercress sandwiches," he was murmuring to himself. "I suppose I must be the only animal of the kind in the world."

"Of course," went on Hyacinth, half to herself, "she might get the people on her side, the ones that she's bribed. And if she did—"

"That's all right, that's all right," said Udo grandly. "Leave her to me. There's something about your water cress that inspires me to terrible deeds. I feel a new—whatever I am."

One gathers reluctantly from this speech that Udo had partaken too freely.

"Of course," said Hyacinth, "I could write to my father, who might send some of his men back, but I shouldn't like to do that. I shouldn't like him to think that I had failed him."

"Extraordinary how I take to these things," said Udo, allowing himself a little more room on the seat. "Perhaps I am a rabbit after all. I wonder what I should look like behind wire netting." He took another bite and went on, "I wonder what I should do if I saw a ferret. I suppose you haven't got a ferret on you, Princess?"

"I beg your pardon, Prince? I'm afraid I was thinking of something else. What did you say?"

"Nothing, nothing. One's thoughts run on." He put his hand out for the plate, and discovered that it was empty. He settled himself more comfortably, and seemed to be about to sink into slumber when his attention was attracted suddenly by the knot in his tail. He picked it up and began lazily to undo it. "I wish I could lash my tail," he murmured; "mine seems to be one of the tails that don't lash." He began very gingerly to feel the tip of it. "I wonder if I've got a sting anywhere." He closed his eyes, muttering, "Sting Countess neck, sting all over neck, sting lots stings," and fell peacefully asleep.

It was a disgraceful exhibition. Roger Scurvilegs tries to slur it over; talks about the great heat of the sun and the notorious effect of even one or two water-cress sandwiches on an empty—on a man who has had nothing to eat for several days. This is to palter with the facts. The effect of water-cress sandwiches upon Udo's arrangements (however furnished) we have all just seen for ourselves; but what Roger neglects to lay stress upon is the fact that it was the effect of twenty-one or twenty-two water-cress sandwiches. There is no denying that it was a disgraceful exhibition. If I had been there, I should certainly have written to his father about it.

Hyacinth looked at him uneasily. Her first feeling was one of sympathy. Poor fellow, she thought, he's had a hard time lately. But it is a strain on the sympathy to gaze too long on a mixture of lion, rabbit, and woolly lamb, particularly when the rabbit part has its mouth open and is snoring gently.

Besides, what could she do with him? She had two of them on her hands now: the Countess and the Prince. Belvane was in an even better position than before. She could now employ Udo to help her in her plots against the Princess. "Grant to me so and so, or I'll keep the enchantment for ever on his Royal Highness." And what could a poor girl do?

Well, she would have to come to some decision in the future. Meanwhile, the difficulties of the moment were enough. The most obvious difficulty was his bedroom. Was it quite the sort of room he wanted now? Hyacinth realized suddenly that to be hostess to such a collection of animals as Udo was would require all the tact she possessed. Perhaps he would tell her what he wanted when he woke up. Better let him sleep peacefully now.

She looked at him, smiled in spite of herself, and went quickly down into the Palace.

13

"Pink" Rhymes with "Think"

UDO AWOKE, SLIGHTLY refreshed, and decided to take a firm line with the Countess at once. He had no difficulty about finding his way down to her. The Palace seemed to be full of servants, all apparently busy about something which brought them for a moment in sight of the newly arrived Prince, and then whisked them off, hand to mouth and shoulders shaking. By one of these, with more control over her countenance than the others, an annoyed Udo was led into Belvane's garden.

She was walking up and down the flagged walk between her lavender hedges, and as he came in, she stopped and rested her elbows on her sundial, and looked mockingly at him, waiting for him to speak. "Between the showers I mark the hours," said the sundial (on the suggestion of Belvane one wet afternoon), but for the moment the Countess was in the way.

"Ah, here we are," said Udo in rather a nasty voice.

"Here we are," said Belvane sweetly. "All of us."

Suddenly she began to laugh.

"Oh, Prince Udo," she said, "you'll be the death of me. Count me as one more of your victims."

It is easy to be angry with anyone who will laugh at you all the time, but difficult to be effective; particularly when—but we need not dwell upon Udo's handicap again.

"I don't see anything to laugh at," he said stiffly. "To intelligent people the outside appearance is not everything."

"But it can be very funny, can't it?" said Belvane coaxingly. "I wished for something humorous to happen to you, but I never thought—"

"Ah," said Udo, "now we've got it."

He spoke with the air of a clever cross-examiner who has skillfully extracted an admission from a reluctant witness. This sort of tone goes best with one of those keen legal faces; perhaps that was why Belvane laughed again.

"You practically confess that you did it," went on Udo magnificently.

"Did what?"

"Turned me into a—a—"

"A rabbit?" said Belvane innocently.

A foolish observation like this always pained Udo.

"What makes you think I'm a rabbit?" he asked.

"I don't mind what you are, but you'll never dare show yourself in the country like this."

"Be careful, woman; don't drive me too far. Beware lest you rouse the lion in me."

"Where?" asked Belvane, with a childlike air.

With a gesture full of dignity and good breeding, Udo called attention to his tail.

"That," said the Countess, "is not the part of the lion that I'm afraid of."

For the moment Udo was nonplussed, but he soon recovered himself.

"Even supposing—just for the sake of argument—that I am a rabbit, I still have something up my sleeve; I'll come and eat your young carnations."

Belvane adored her garden, but she was sustained by the thought that it was only July now. She pointed this out to him.

"It needn't necessarily be carnations," he warned her.

"I don't want to put my opinion against one who has (forgive me) inside knowledge on the subject, but I think I have nothing in my garden at this moment that would agree with a rabbit."

"I don't mind if it *doesn't* agree with me," said Udo heroically.

This was more serious. Her dear garden in which she composed, ruined by the mastications—machinations—what was the word?—of an enemy! The thought was unbearable.

"You aren't a rabbit," she said hastily; "you aren't really a rabbit. Because—because you don't *woffle* your nose properly."

"I could," said Udo simply. "I'm just keeping it back, that's all."

"Show me how," cried Belvane, clasping her hands eagerly together.

It was not what he had come into the garden for, and it accorded ill with the dignity of the Royal House of Araby, but somehow one got led on by this wicked woman.

"Like this," said Udo.

The Countess looked at him critically with her head on one side.

"No," she said, "that's quite wrong."

"Naturally I'm a little out of practice."

"I'm sorry," said Belvane. "I'm afraid I can't pass you."

Udo couldn't think what had happened to the conversation. With a great effort he extracted himself from it.

"Enough of this, Countess," he said sternly. "I have your admission that it was you who put this enchantment on me."

"It was I. I wasn't going to have you here interfering with my plans."

"Your plans to rob the Princess."

Belvane felt that it was useless to explain the principles of largesse-throwing to Udo. There will always be men like Udo and Roger Scurvilegs who take these narrow matter-of-fact views. One merely wastes time in arguing with them.

"My plans," she repeated.

"Very well. I shall go straight to the Princess, and she will unmask you before the people."

Belvane smiled happily. One does not often get such a chance.

"And who," she asked sweetly, "will unmask your Royal Highness before the people, so that they may see the true Prince Udo underneath?"

"What do you mean?" said Udo, though he was beginning to guess.

"That noble handsome countenance which is so justly the pride of Araby—how shall we show that to the people? They'll form such a mistaken idea of it if they all see you like this, won't they?"

Udo was quite sure now that he understood. Hyacinth had understood at the very beginning.

"You mean that if the Princess Hyacinth falls in with your plans, you will restore me to my proper form, but that otherwise you will leave me like this?"

"One's actions are very much misunderstood." Belvane sighed. "I've no doubt that that is how it will appear to future historians."

(To Roger, certainly.)

It was too much for Udo. He forgot his manners and made a jump toward her. She glided gracefully behind the sundial in a pretty affectation of alarm . . . and the next moment Udo decided that the contest between them was not to be settled by such rough-and-tumble methods as these. The fact that his tail had caught in something helped him to decide.

Belvane was up to him in an instant.

"There, there!" she said soothingly. "Let *me* undo it for your Royal Highness." She talked pleasantly as she worked at it. "Every little accident teaches us something. Now if you'd been a rabbit, this wouldn't have happened."

"No, I'm not even a rabbit," said Undo sadly. "I'm just nothing."

Belvane stood up and made him a deep curtsy.

"You are his Royal Highness Prince Udo of Araby. Your Royal Highness's straw is prepared. When will your Royal Highness be pleased to retire?"

It was a little unkind, I think. I should not record it of her were not Roger so insistent.

"Now," said Udo, and lolloped sadly off. It was his one really dignified moment in Euralia.

On his way to his apartment he met Wiggs.

"Wiggs," he said solemnly, "if ever you can do anything to annoy that woman, such as making her an apple pie bed, or *anything* like that, I wish you'd do it."

Whereupon he retired for the night. Into the mysteries of his toilet we had perhaps better not inquire.

As the chronicler of these simple happenings many years ago, it is my duty to be impartial. "These are the facts," I should say, "and it is for your nobilities to judge of them. Thus and thus my characters acted; how say you, my lords and ladies?"

I confess that this attitude is beyond me; I have a fondness for all my people, and I would not have you misunderstand any of them. But with regard to one of them there is no need for me to say anything in her defense. About her at any rate we agree.

I mean Wiggs. We take the same view as Hyacinth: she was the best little girl in Euralia. It will come then as a shock to you (as it did to me on the morning after I had staggered home with Roger's seventeen volumes) to learn that on her day Wiggs could be as bad as anybody. I mean really bad. To tear your frock, to read books which you ought to be dusting, these are accidents which may happen to anybody. Far otherwise was Wiggs's fall.

She adopted, in fact, the infamous suggestion of Prince Udo. Three nights later, with malice aforethought and to the comfort of the King's enemies and the prejudice of the safety of the realm, she made an apple-pie bed for the Countess.

It was the most perfect apple-pie bed ever made. Cox himself could not have improved upon it; Newton has seen nothing like it. It took Wiggs a whole morning; and the results, though private (that is the worst of an apple-pie bed), were beyond expectation. After wrestling for half an hour the Countess spent the night in a garden hammock, composing a bitter "Ode to Melancholy."

Of course Wiggs caught it in the morning; the Countess suspected what she could not prove. Wiggs, now in for a thoroughly bad week, realized that it was her turn again. What should she do?

An inspiration came to her. She had been really bad the day before; it was a pity to waste such perfect badness as that. Why not have the one bad wish to which the ring entitled her?

She drew the ring out from its hiding place round her neck.

"I wish," she said, holding it up, "I wish that the Countess Belvane"—she stopped to think of something that would really annoy her—"I wish that the Countess shall never be able to write another rhyme again."

She held her breath, expecting a thunderclap or some other outward token of the sudden death of Belvane's muse. Instead she was struck by the extraordinary silence of the place. She had a horrid feeling that everybody else was dead, and realizing all at once that she was a very wicked little girl, she ran up to her room and gave herself up to tears.

MAY YOU, DEAR SIR OR MADAM, REPENT AS QUICKLY!

However, this is not a moral work. An hour later Wiggs came into Belvane's garden, eager to discover in what way her inability to rhyme would manifest itself. It seemed that she had chosen the exact moment.

In the throes of composition Belvane had quite forgotten the apple-pie bed, so absorbing is our profession. She welcomed Wiggs eagerly, and taking her hand, led her toward the roses.

"I have just been talking to my dear roses," she said. "Listen:

" 'Whene'er I take my walks about,
I like to see the roses out;
I like them yellow, white, and pink,
But crimson are the best, I think.
The butterfly—' "

But we shall never know about the butterfly. It may be that Wiggs has lost us here a thought on lepidoptera which the world can ill spare, for she interrupted breathlessly.

"When did you write that?"

"I was just making it up when you came in, dear child. These thoughts often come to me as I walk up and down my beautiful garden. "The butterfly . . .' "

But Wiggs had let go her hand and was running back to the Palace. She wanted to be alone to think this out.

What had happened? That it was truly a magic ring, as the fairy had told her, she had no doubt; that her wish was a bad one, that she had been bad enough to earn it, she was equally certain. What then had happened? There was only one answer to her question. The bad wish had been granted to somebody else.

To whom? She had lent the ring to nobody. True, she had told the Princess all about it, but . . .

Suddenly she remembered. The Countess had had it in her hands for a moment. Yes, and she had sent her out of the room, and . . .

So many thoughts crowded into Wiggs's mind at this moment that she felt she must share them with somebody. She ran off to find the Princess.

14

"Why Can't You Be Like Wiggs?"

HYACINTH WAS WITH Udo in the library. Udo spent much of his time in the library nowadays; for surely in one of those many books was to be found some Advice to a Gentleman in Temporary Difficulties suitable to a case like his. Hyacinth kept him company sadly. It had been such a brilliant idea inviting him to Euralia; how she wished now that she had never done it.

"Well, Wiggs," she said, with a gentle smile, "what have you been doing with yourself all the morning?"

Udo looked up from his mat and nodded to her.

"I've found out," said Wiggs excitedly; "it was the *Countess* who did it."

Udo surveyed her with amazement.

"The Princess Hyacinth," he said, "has golden hair. One discovers these things gradually." And he returned to his book.

Wiggs looked bewildered.

"He means, dear," said Hyacinth, "that it is quite obvious that the Countess did it, and we have known about it for days."

Udo wore, as far as his face would permit, the slightly puffy expression of one who has just said something profoundly ironical and is feeling self-conscious about it.

"Oh—h," said Wiggs in such a disappointed voice that it seemed as if she were going to cry.

Hyacinth, like the dear that she was, made haste to comfort her.

"We didn't really *know*," she said; "we only guessed it. But now that you have found out, I shall be able to punish her properly. No, don't come with me," she said, as she rose and moved toward the door; "stay here and help his Royal Highness. Perhaps you can find the book that he wants; you've read more of them than I have, I expect."

Left alone with the Prince, Wiggs was silent for a little, looking at him rather anxiously.

"Do you know *all* about the Countess?" she asked at last.

"If there's anything I don't know, it must be *very* bad."

"Then you know that it's all my fault that you are like this? Oh, dear Prince Udo, I am so dreadfully sorry."

"What do you mean—*your* fault?"

"Because it was my ring that did it."

Udo scratched his head in a slightly puzzled but quite a nice way.

"Tell me all about it from the beginning," he said. "You have found out something after all, I believe."

So Wiggs told her story from the beginning. How the fairy had given her a ring; how the Countess had taken it from her for five minutes and had a bad wish on it; and how Wiggs had found her out that very morning.

Udo was intensely excited by the story. He trotted up and down the library, muttering to himself. He stopped in front of Wiggs as soon as she had finished.

"Is the ring still going?" he asked. "I mean, can you have another wish on it?"

"Yes, just one."

"Then wish her to be turned into a . . ." He tried to think of something that would meet the case. "What about a spider?" he said thoughtfully.

"But that's a *bad* wish," said Wiggs.

"Yes, but it's *her* turn."

"Oh, but I'm only allowed a good wish now." She added rapturously, "And I know what it's going to be."

So did Udo. At least he thought he did.

"Oh, you dear," he said, casting an affectionate look upon her.

"Yes, that's it. That I may be able to dance like a fairy."

Udo could hardly believe his ears, and they were adequate enough for most emergencies.

"But how is that going to help *me?*" he said, tapping his chest with his paw.

"But it's *my* ring," said Wiggs. "And so of course I'm going to wish that I can dance like a fairy. I've always meant to, as soon as I've been good for a day first."

The child was absurdly selfish. Udo saw that he would have to appeal to her in another way.

"Of course," he began, "I've nothing to say against dancing *as* dancing, but I think you'll get tired of it. Just as I shall get tired of—lettuce."

Wiggs understood now.

"You mean that I might wish you to be a Prince again?"

"Well," said Udo casually, "it just occurred to me as an example of what might be called the Good Wish."

"Then I shall never be able to dance like a fairy?"

"Neither shall I, if it comes to that," said Udo. Really, the child was very stupid.

"Oh, it's too cruel," said Wiggs, stamping her foot. "I did so want to be able to dance."

Udo glanced gloomily into the future.

"To live forever behind wire netting," he mused; "to be eternally frightened by pink-eyed ferrets; to be offered bran mash—bran mash—bran mash wherever one visited, week after week, month after month, year after year, century after—how long *do* rabbits live."

But Wiggs was not to be moved.

"I *won't* give up my wish," she said passionately.

Udo got on to his four legs with dignity.

"Keep your wish," he said. "There are plenty of other ways of getting out of enchantments. I'll learn up a piece of poetry by our Court Poet Sacharino, and recite it backward when the moon is new. Something like that. I can do this quite easily by myself. Keep your wish."

He went slowly out. His tail (looking more like a bell rope than ever) followed him solemnly. The fluffy part that you pull was for a moment left behind; then with a jerk it was gone, and Wiggs was left alone.

"I won't give up my wish," cried Wiggs again. "I'll wish it now before I'm sorry." She held the ring up. "I wish that . . ." She stopped suddenly. "Poor Prince Udo, he seems very unhappy. I wonder if it *is* a good wish to wish to dance when people are unhappy." She thought this out for a little, and then made her great resolve. "Yes," she said, "I'll wish him well again."

Once more she held the ring up in her two hands.

"I wish," she said, "that Prince Udo . . ."

I know what you are going to say. It was no good her wishing her good wish, because she had been a bad girl the day before—making the Countess an apple-pie bed and all—disgraceful! How could she possibly suppose . . .

She didn't. She remembered just in time.

"Oh, bother," said Wiggs, standing in the middle of the room with the ring held above her head. "I've got to be good for a day first. *Bother!*"

So the next day was Wiggs's Good Day. The legend of it was handed down for years afterwards in Euralia. It got into all the Calendars—July Twentieth, it was—marked with a red star; in Roger's portentous volumes it had a chapter devoted to it. There was some talk about it being made into a public holiday, he tells us, but this fell through. Euralian mothers used to scold their naughty children with the words, "Why can't you be like Wiggs?" and the children used to tell each other that there never was a real Wiggs, and that it was only a made-up story for parents. However, you have my word for it that it was true.

She began by getting up at five o'clock in the morning, and after dressing herself very neatly (and being particularly careful to wring out her sponge), she made her own bed and tidied up the room. For a moment she thought of waking the grownups in the Palace and letting them enjoy the beautiful morning too, but a little reflection showed her that this would not be at all a kindly act; so, having dusted the Throne Room and performed a few simple physical exercises, she went outside and attended to the smaller domestic animals.

At breakfast she had three helps of something very nutritious, which the Countess said would make her grow, but only one help of everything else. She sat up nicely all the time, and never pointed to anything or drank with her mouth full. After breakfast she scattered some crumbs on the lawn for the robins, and then got to work again.

First she dusted and dusted and dusted; then she swept and swept and swept; then she sewed and sewed and sewed. When anybody of superior station or age came into the room she rose and curtsied and stood with her hands behind her back while she was being spoken to. When anybody said, "I wonder where I put my so-and-so," she jumped up and said, "Let *me* fetch it," even if it was upstairs.

After dinner she made up a basket of provisions and took them to the old women who lived near the castle; to some of them she sang or read aloud, and when at one cottage she was asked, "Now won't you give me a little dance?"

she smiled bravely and said, "I'm afraid I don't dance very well." I think that was rather sweet of her; if I had been the fairy I should have let her off the rest of the day.

When she got back to the Palace she drank two glasses of warm milk, with the skin on, and then went and weeded the Countess's lawn; and once when she trod by accident on a bed of flowers, she left the footprint there instead of scraping it over hastily, and pretending that she hadn't been near the place, as you would have done.

And at half past six she kissed everybody good night (including Udo) and went to bed.

So ended July the Twentieth, perhaps the most memorable day in Euralian history.

Udo and Hyacinth spent the great day peacefully in the library. A gentleman for all his fur, Udo had not told the Princess about Wiggs's refusal to help him. Besides, a man has his dignity. To be turned into a mixture of three animals by a woman of thirty, and to be turned back again by a girl of ten, is to be too much the plaything of the sex. It was time he did something for himself.

"Now then, how did that bit of Sacharino's go? Let me see." He beat time with a paw. " 'Blood for something, something, something. He who something, something, some . . .' Some-

thing like that. 'Blood for—er—blood for—er
. . .' No, it's gone again. I know there was a bit
of blood in it."

"I'm sure you'll get it soon," said Hyacinth.
"It sounds as though it's going to be just the
sort of thing that's wanted."

"Oh, I shall get it all right. Some of the words
have escaped me for the moment, that's all.
'Blood—er—blood.' You must have heard of it,
Princess: it's about blood for he who something; you must know the one I mean."

"I know I've heard of it," said the Princess,
wrinkling her forehead, "only I can't quite think
of it for the moment. It's about a—a—"

"Yes, that's it," said Udo.

Then they both looked up at the ceiling with
their heads on one side and murmured to themselves.

But noon came and still they hadn't thought
of it.

After a simple meal they returned to the
library.

"I think I'd better write to Coronel," said
Udo, "and ask him about it."

"I thought you said his name was Sacharino."

"Oh, this is not the poet, it's just a friend of
mine, but he's rather good at this sort of thing.
The trouble is that it takes such a long time for
a letter to get there and back."

At the word "letter," Hyacinth started suddenly.

"Oh, Prince Udo," she cried, "I can never forgive myself. I've just remembered the very thing. Father told me in his letter that a little couplet he once wrote was being very useful for—er—removing things."

"What sort of things?" said Udo, not too hopefully.

"Oh, enchantments and things."

Udo was a little annoyed at the "and things" —as though turning him back into a Prince again was as much in the day's work as removing rust from a helmet.

"It goes like this," said Hyacinth.

> " 'Bo, boll, bill, bole.
> Wo, woll, will, wole.'

"It sounds as though it would remove *anything*," she added, with a smile.

Udo sat up rather eagerly.

"I'll try," he said. "Is there any particular action goes with it?"

"I've never heard of any. I expect you ought to say it as if you meant it."

Udo sat up on his back paws, and, gesticulating freely with his right paw, declaimed:

> " 'Bo, boll, bill, bole.
> Wo, woll, will, wole.' "

He fixed his eyes on his paws, waiting for the transformation.

He waited.

And waited.

Nothing happened.

"It must be all right," said Hyacinth anxiously, "because I'm sure Father would know. Try saying it more like this."

She repeated the lines in a voice so melting, yet withal so dignified, that the very chairs might have been expected to get up and walk out.

Udo imitated her as well as he could.

At about the time when Wiggs was just falling asleep, he repeated it in his fiftieth different voice.

"I'm sorry," said Hyacinth; "perhaps it isn't so good as Father thought it was."

"There's just one chance," said Udo. "It's possible it may have to be said on an empty stomach. I'll try it tomorrow before breakfast."

Upstairs Wiggs was dreaming of the dancing that she had given up forever.

And what Belvane was doing, I really don't know.

15

There Is a Lover Waiting for Hyacinth

SO THE NEXT morning before breakfast Wiggs went up on to the castle walls and wished. She looked over the meadows, and across the peaceful stream that wandered through them, to the forest where she had first met her fairy, and she gave a little sigh. "Goodbye, dancing," she said; and then she held the ring up and went on bravely, "Please, I was a very good girl all yesterday, and I wish that Prince Udo may be well again."

For a full minute there was silence. Then from the direction of Udo's room below there came these remarkable words:

"*Take the beastly stuff away, and bring me a beefsteak and a flagon of sack!*"

Between smiles and tears Wiggs murmured, "He *sounds* all right. I *am* g—glad."

And then she could bear it no longer. She

hurried down and out of the Palace—away, away from Udo and the Princess and the Countess and all their talk, to the cool friendly forest, there to be alone and to think over all that she had lost.

It was very quiet in the forest. At the foot of her own favourite tree, a veteran of many hundred summers who stood sentinel over an open glade that dipped to a gurgling brook and climbed gently away from it, she sat down. On the soft green yonder she might have danced, an enchanted place, and now—never, never, never. . . .

How long had she sat there? It must have been a long time—because the forest had been so quiet, and now it was so full of sound. The trees were murmuring something to her, and the birds were singing it, and the brook was trying to tell it, too, but would keep chuckling over the very idea so that you could hardly hear what it was saying, and there were rustlings in the grass—"Get up, get up," everything was calling to her; "dance, dance."

She got up, a little frightened. Everything seemed so strangely beautiful. She had never felt it like this before. Yes, she would dance. She must say "Thank you" for all this somehow; perhaps they would excuse her if it was not very well expressed.

"This will just be for 'Thank you,'" she said as she got up. "I shall never dance again."

And then she danced. . . .

Where are you, Hyacinth? There is a lover waiting for you somewhere, my dear.

It is the first of spring. The blackbird opens his yellow beak and whistles cool and clear. There is blue magic in the morning; the sky, deep-blue above, melts into white where it meets the hills. The wind waits for you up yonder— will you go to meet it? Ah, stay here! The hedges have put on their green coats for you; misty green are the tall elms from which the rooks are chattering. Along the clean white road, between the primrose banks, he comes. Will you be round this corner?—or the next? He is looking for you, Hyacinth.

(She rested, breathless, and then danced again.)

It is summer afternoon. All the village is at rest save one. "Cuck-oo!" comes from the deep dark trees; "Cuck-oo!" he calls again, and flies away to send back the answer. The fields, all green and gold, sleep undisturbed by the full river which creeps along them. The air is heavy with the scent of May. Where are you, Hyacinth? Is not this the trysting place? I have waited for you so long! . . .

She stopped, and the watcher in the bushes moved silently away, his mind aflame with fancies.

Wiggs went back to the Palace to tell everybody that she could dance.

*   *   *

"Shall we tell her how it happened?" said Udo jauntily. "I just recited a couple of lines—poetry, you know—backward, and—well, here I am!"

"O—oh!" said Wiggs.

16

Belvane Enjoys Herself

THE ENTRANCE OF an attendant into his room that morning to bring him his early bran mash had awakened Udo. As soon as she was gone he jumped up, shook the straw from himself, and said in a very passion of longing,

> " 'Bo, boll, bill, bole.
> Wo, woll, will wole.' "

He felt that it was his last chance. Exhausted by his effort, he fell back on the straw and dropped asleep again. It was nearly an hour later that he became properly awake.

Into his feelings I shall not enter at any length; I leave that to Roger Scurvilegs. Between ourselves Roger is a bit of a snob. The degradation to a Prince of Araby to be turned into an animal so ludicrous, the delight of a Prince of Araby at

161

regaining his own form, it is this that he chiefly dwells upon. Really, I think you or I would have been equally delighted. I am sure we can guess how Udo felt about it.

He strutted about the room, he gazed at himself in every glass, he held out his hand to an imaginary Hyacinth with "Ah, dear Princess, and how are we this morning?" Never had he felt so handsome and so sure of himself. It was in the middle of one of his pirouettings that he caught sight of the unfortunate bran mash, and uttered the remarkable words which I have already recorded.

The actual meeting with Hyacinth was even better than he had expected. Hardly able to believe that it was true, she seized his hands impulsively and cried: "Oh, Prince Udo! oh, my dear, I *am* so glad!"

Udo twirled his moustache and felt a very gay dog indeed.

At breakfast (where Udo did himself extremely well) they discussed plans. The first thing was to summon the Countess into their presence. An attendant was sent to fetch her.

"If you would like me to conduct the interview," said Udo, "I've no doubt that—"

"I think I shall be all right now that you are with me. I shan't feel so afraid of her now."

The attendant came in again.

"Her ladyship is not yet down, your Royal Highness."

"Tell her that I wish to see her directly she *is* down," said the Princess.

The attendant withdrew.

"You were telling me about this army of hers," said Udo. "One of my ideas—I had a good many while I was—er—in retirement—was that she could establish the Army properly at her own expense, and that she herself should be perpetual Orderly-sergeant."

"Isn't that a nice thing to be?" asked Hyacinth innocently.

"It's a *horrible* thing to be. Another of my ideas was that—"

The attendant came in again.

"Her ladyship is a little indisposed, and is staying in bed for the present."

"Oh! Did her ladyship say when she thought of getting up?"

"Her ladyship didn't seem to think of getting up at all today. Her ladyship told me to say that she didn't seem to know *when* she'd get up again."

The attendant withdrew, and Hyacinth and Udo, standing together in a corner, discussed the matter anxiously.

"I don't quite see what we can *do*," said Hyacinth. "We can't *pull* her out of bed. Besides, she may really be ill. Supposing she stays there forever!"

"Of course," said Udo. "It would be rather—"

"You see if we—"

"We might possibly—"

"*Good* morning, all!" said Belvane, sweeping into the room. She dropped a profound curtsy to the Princess. "Your Royal Highness! And dear Prince Udo, looking his own charming self again!"

She had made a superb toilet. In her flowing gold brocade, cut square in front to reveal the whitest of necks, with her black hair falling in two braids to her knees and twined with pearls which were caught up in loops at her waist, she looked indeed a Queen; while Hyacinth and Udo, taken utterly by surprise, seemed to be two conspirators whom she had caught in the act of plotting against her.

"I—I thought you weren't well, Countess," said Hyacinth, trying to recover herself.

"I, not well?" cried Belvane, clasping her hands to her breast. "I thought it was his Royal Highness who . . . Ah, but he's looking a true Prince now."

She turned her eyes upon him, and there was in that look so much of admiration, humour, appeal, impudence—I don't know what (and Roger cannot tell us, either)—that Udo forgot entirely what he was going to say and could only gaze at her in wonder.

Her mere entry had dazzled him. There is no knowing with a woman like Balvane; and I believe that she had purposely kept herself plain during these last few days so that she might have the weapon of her beauty to fall back upon in case anything went wrong. Things had indeed gone wrong; Udo had become a man again, and it was against the man that this last weapon was directed.

Udo himself was only too ready. The fact that he was once more attractive to women meant as much as anything to him. To have been attractive to Hyacinth would have contented most of us, but Udo felt a little uncomfortable with her. He could not forget the last few days, nor the fact that he had once been an object of pity to her. Now Belvane had not pitied him.

Hyacinth had got control of herself by this time.

"Enough of this, Countess," she said with dignity. "We have not forgotten the treason which you were plotting against the State; we have not forgotten your base attack upon our guest, Prince Udo. I order you now to remain within the confines of the Palace until we shall have decided what to do with you. You may leave us."

Belvane dropped her eyes meekly.

"I am at your Royal Highness's commands. I shall be in my garden when your Royal Highness wants me."

She raised her eyes, gave one fleeting glance to Prince Udo, and withdrew.

"A hateful woman," said Hyacinth. "What shall we do with her?"

"I think," said Udo, "that I had better speak to her seriously first. I have no doubt that I can drag from her the truth of her conspiracy against you. There may be many others in it, in which case we shall have to proceed with caution; on the other hand, it may be just misplaced zeal on her part, in which case—"

"Was it misplaced zeal which made her turn you into a . . ."

Udo held up his hand hastily.

"I have not forgotten that," he said. "Be sure that I shall exact full reparation. Let me see; *which* is the way to her garden?"

Hyacinth did not know quite what to make of her guest. At the moment when she first saw him in his proper form, the improvement on his late appearance had been so marked that he had seemed almost the handsome young Prince of her dreams. Every minute after that had detracted from him. His face was too heavy, his manner was too pompous; one of these days he would be too fat.

Moreover, he was just a little too sure of his position in her house. She had wanted his help, but she did not want so much of it as she seemed to be likely to get.

Udo, feeling that it was going to be rather a nice day, went into Belvane's garden. He had been there once before; it seemed to him a very much prettier garden this morning, and the woman who was again awaiting him, much more desirable.

Belvane made room for him on the seat next her.

"This is where I sit when I write my poetry," she said. "I don't know if your Royal Highness is fond of poetry?"

"Extremely," said Udo. "I have never actually written any or indeed read much, but I have a great admiration for those who—er—admire it. But it was not to talk about poetry that I came out here, Countess."

"No?" said Belvane. "But your Royal Highness must have read the works of Sacharino, the famous bard of Araby?"

"Sacharino, of course. 'Blood for something, something. . . . He who something. . . .' I mean, it's a delightful little thing. Everybody knows it. But it was to talk about something very different that I—"

> " 'Blood for blood and shoon for shoon,
> He who runs may read my rune,' "

quoted Belvane softly. "It is perhaps Sacharino's most perfect gem."

"That's it," cried Udo excitedly. "I knew I knew it, if only I could . . ." He broke off suddenly, remembering the circumstances in which he had wanted it. He coughed importantly and explained for the third time that he had not come to talk to her about poetry.

"But of course I think his most noble poem of all," went on Belvane, apparently misunderstanding him, "is the ode to your Royal Highness upon your coming of age. Let me see, how does it begin?

" 'Prince Udo, so dashing and bold,
      Is apparently eighteen years old.
      It is eighteen years since
      This wonderful Prince
      Was born in the Palace, I'm told.' "

"These Court Poets," said Udo, with an air of unconcern, "flatter one, of course."

If he expected a compliment he was disappointed.

"There I cannot judge," said Belvane, "until I know your Royal Highness better." She looked at him out of the corner of her eye. "Is your Royal Highness very—dashing?"

"I—er—well—er—one—that is to say . . ." He waded on uncomfortably, feeling less dashing every moment. He should have realized at once that it was an impossible question to answer.

"Your Royal Highness," said Belvane modestly, "must not be too dashing with us poor Euralians."

For the fourth time Udo explained that he had come there to speak to her severely, and that Belvane seemed to have mistaken his purpose.

"Oh, forgive me, Prince Udo," she begged. "I quite thought that you had come out to commune soul to soul with a fellow lover of the beautiful."

"N—no," said Udo; "not exactly."

"Then what is it?" she cried, clasping her hands eagerly together. "I know it will be something exciting."

Udo stood up. He felt that he could be more severe a little farther off. He moved a few yards away, and then turned round toward her, resting his elbow on the sundial.

"Countess," he began sternly, "ten days ago, as I was starting on my journey hither, I was suddenly—"

"Just a moment," said Belvane, whispering eagerly to herself rather than to him, and she jumped up with a cushion from the seat where she was sitting, and ran across and arranged it under his elbow. "He would have been *so* uncomfortable," she murmured, and she hurried back to her seat again and sat down and gazed at him, with her elbows on her knees and her chin resting on her hands. "Now go on telling me," she said breathlessly.

Udo opened his mouth with the obvious intention of obeying her, but no words came. He seemed to have lost the thread of his argument. He felt a perfect fool, stuck up there with his elbow on a cushion, just as if he were addressing a public meeting. He looked at his elbow as if he expected to find a glass of water there ready, and Belvane divined his look and made a movement as if she were about to get it for him. It would be just like her. He flung the cushion from him ("Oh, mind my roses," cried Belvane) and came down angrily to her. Belvane looked at him with wide, innocent eyes.

"You—you—oh, *don't* look like that!"

"Like that?" said Belvane, looking like it again.

"Don't *do* it," shouted Udo, and he turned and kicked the cushion down the flagged path. "Stop it."

Belvane stopped it.

"Do you know," she said, "I'm rather frightened of you when you're angry with me."

"I *am* angry. Very, very angry. Excessively annoyed."

"I thought you were." She sighed.

"And you know very well why."

She nodded her head at him.

"It's my dreadful temper," she said. "I do such thoughtless things when I lose my temper."

She sighed again, and looked meekly at the ground.

170

"Er, well, you shouldn't," said Udo weakly.

"It was the slight to my sex that made me so angry. I couldn't bear to think that we women couldn't rule ourselves for such a short time, and that a man had to be called in to help us." She looked up at him shyly. "Of course I didn't know then what the man was going to be like. But now that I know . . ."

Suddenly she held her arms out to him beseechingly.

"Stay with us, Prince Udo, and help us! Men are so wise, so brave, so—so generous. They know nothing of the little petty feelings of revenge that women indulge."

"Really, Countess, we—er—you—eh . . . Of course there is good deal in what you say, and I—er—"

"Won't you sit down again, Prince Udo?"

Udo sat down next to her.

"And now," said Belvane, "let's talk it over comfortably, as friends should."

"Of course," began Udo, "I quite see your point. You hadn't seen me; you didn't know anything about me: to you I might have been just any man."

"I knew a little about you when you came here. Beneath the—er—outward mask I saw how brave and dignified you were. But even if I could have got you back to your proper form again, I think I should have been afraid to;

because I didn't know then how generous, how forgiving, you were."

It seemed to be quite decided that Udo was forgiving her. When a very beautiful woman thanks you humbly for something you have not yet given her, there is only one thing for a gentleman to do. Udo patted her hand reassuringly.

"Oh, thank you, your Royal Highness." She gave herself a little shake and jumped up. "And now shall I show you my beautiful garden?"

"A garden with you in it, dear Countess, is always beautiful," he said gallantly. And it was not bad, I think, for a man who had been living on water cress and bran mash only the day before.

They wandered round the garden together. Udo was now quite certain it was going to be a nice day.

It was an hour later when he came into the library. Hyacinth greeted him eagerly.

"Well?" she said.

Udo nodded his head wisely.

"I have spoken to her about her conduct to me," he said. "There will be no more trouble in that direction, I fancy. She explained her conduct to me very fully, and I have decided to overlook it this time."

"But her robberies, her plots, her conspiracy against *me!*"

Udo looked blankly at her for a moment, and then pulled himself together.

"I am speaking to her about that this afternoon," he said.

17

The King of Barodia Drops the Whisker Habit

KING MERRIWIG SAT in his tent, his head held well back, his eyes gazing upward. His rubicund cheeks were for the moment a snowy white. A hind of the name of Carlo had him firmly by the nose. Yet King Merriwig neither struggled nor protested; he was, in fact, being shaved.

The Court Barber was in his usual conversational mood. He released his Majesty's nose for a moment, and as he turned to sharpen his razor, remarked, "Terrible war, this."

"Terrible," agreed the King.

"Don't seem no end to it, like."

"Well, well," said Merriwig, "we shall see."

The barber got to work again.

"Do you know what I should do to the King of Barodia if I had him here?"

Merriwig did not dare to speak, but he indicated with his right eye that he was interested in the conversation.

"I'd shave his whiskers off," said Carlo firmly.

The King gave a sudden jerk, and for the moment there were signs of a battle upon the snow; then the King leaned back again, and in another minute or so the operation was over.

"It will soon be all right," said Carlo, mopping at his Majesty's chin. "Your Majesty shouldn't have moved."

"It was my own fault, Carlo; you gave me a sudden idea, that's all."

"You're welcome, your Majesty."

As soon as he was gone, the King took out his tablets. On these he was accustomed to record any great thoughts which occurred to him during the day. He now wrote in them these noble words:

"Jewels of wisdom may fall from the meanest of hinds."

He struck a gong to summon the Chancellor into his presence.

"I have a great idea," he told the Chancellor.

The Chancellor hid his surprise and expressed his pleasure.

"Tonight I propose to pay a secret visit to his Majesty the King of Barodia. Which of the many tents yonder have my spies located as the royal one?"

"The big one in the centre, above which the Royal Arms fly."

"I thought as much. Indeed, I have often seen his Majesty entering it. But one prefers to do these things according to the custom. Acting on the information given me by my trusty spies, I propose to enter the King of Barodia's tent at dead of night, and . . ."

The Chancellor shuddered in anticipation.

". . . and shave his whiskers off."

The Chancellor trembled with delight.

"Your Majesty," he said in a quavering voice, "forty years, man and boy, have I served your Majesty, and your Majesty's late lamented father, and never have I heard such a beautiful plan."

Merriwig struggled with himself for a moment, but his natural honesty was too much for him.

"It was put into my head by a remark of my Court Barber's," he said casually. "But of course the actual working out of it has been mine."

"Jewels of wisdom," said the Chancellor sententiously, "may fall from the meanest of hinds."

"I suppose," said Merriwig, taking up his tablets and absently scratching out the words written thereon, "there is nothing in the rules against it?"

"By no means, your Majesty. In the annals of Euralia there are many instances of humour similar to that which your Majesty suggests: humour, if I may say so, which, while evidencing to the ignorant only the lighter side of war, has its roots in the most fundamental strategical considerations."

Merriwig regarded him with admiration. This was indeed a Chancellor.

"The very words," he answered, "which I said to myself when the idea came to me. 'The fact,' I said, 'that this will help us to win the war must not disguise from us the fact that the King of Barodia will look extremely funny without his whiskers.' Tonight I shall sally forth and put my plan into practice."

At midnight, then, he started out. The Chancellor awaited his return with some anxiety. This might well turn out to be the decisive stroke (or strokes) of the war. For centuries past the ruling monarchs of Barodia had been famous for their ginger whiskers. "As lost as the King of Barodia without his whiskers," was, indeed, a proverb of those times. A King without a pair, and at such a crisis in his country's fortunes! It was inconceivable. At the least he would have to live in retirement until they grew again, and without the leadership of their King, the Barodian army would become a rabble.

The Chancellor was not distressed at the thought; he was looking forward to his return to Euralia, where he kept a comfortable house. It was not that his life in the field was uninteresting; he had as much work to do as any man.

It was part of his business, for instance, to test the pretentions of any new wizard or spell-monger who was brought into the camp. Such-and-such a quack would seek an interview on the pretext that for five hundred crowns he could turn the King of Barodia into a small black pig. He would be brought before the Chancellor.

"You say that you can turn a man into a small black pig?" the Chancellor would ask.

"Yes, your lordship. It came to me from my grandmother."

"Then turn me," the Chancellor would say simply.

The so-called wizard would try. As soon as the incantation was over, the Chancellor surveyed himself in the mirror. Then he nodded to a couple of soldiers, and the impostor was tied backward on to a mule and driven with jeers out of the camp. There were many such impostors (who at least made a mule out of it), and the Chancellor's life did not lack excitement.

But he yearned now for the simple comforts of his home. He liked pottering about his garden when his work at the Palace was finished; he liked, over the last meal of the day, to tell his wife all the important things he had been doing since he had seen her, and to impress her with the fact that he was the holder of many state secrets which she must not attempt to drag from him. A woman of less tact would have considered the subject closed at this point, but she knew that he was only longing to be persuaded. However, as she always found the secrets too dull to tell anyone else, no great harm was done.

"Just help me off with this cloak," said a voice in front of him.

The Chancellor felt about until his hands encountered a solid body. He undid the cloak and the King stood revealed before him.

"Thanks. Well, I've done it. It went to my heart to do it at the last moment, so beautiful they were, but I nerved myself to it. Poor soul, he slept like a lamb through it all. I wonder what he'll say when he wakes up."

"Did you bring them back with you?" asked the Chancellor excitedly.

"My dear Chancellor, what a question!" He produced them from his pocket. "In the morning we'll run them up on the flagstaff for all Barodia to see."

"He won't like that," said the Chancellor, chuckling.

"I don't quite see what he can do about it," said Merriwig.

The King of Barodia didn't quite see, either.

A fit of sneezing woke him up that morning, and at the same moment he felt a curious draught about his cheeks. He put his hand up and immediately knew the worst.

"Hullo, there!" he bellowed to the sentry outside the door.

"Your Majesty," said the sentry, coming in with alacrity.

The King bobbed down again at once.

"Send the Chancellor to me," said an angry voice from under the bedclothes.

When the Chancellor came in, it was to see the back only of his august monarch.

"Chancellor," said the King, "prepare yourself for a shock."

"Yes, sir," said the Chancellor, trembling exceedingly.

"You are about to see something which no man in the history of Barodia has ever seen before."

The Chancellor, not having the least idea what to expect, waited nervously. The next moment the tent seemed to swim before his eyes, and he knew no more. . . .

When he came to, the King was pouring a jug of water down his neck and murmuring rough words of comfort in his ear.

"Oh, your Majesty," said the poor Chancellor, "your Majesty! I don't know what to say, your Majesty." He mopped at himself as he spoke, and the water trickled from him on to the floor.

"Pull yourself together," said the King sternly. "We shall want all your wisdom, which is notoriously not much, to help us in this crisis."

"Your Majesty, who has dared to do this grievous thing?"

"You fool, how should I know? Do you think they did it while I was awake?"

The Chancellor stiffened a little. He was accustomed to being called a fool; but that was by a man with a terrifying pair of ginger whiskers. From the rather fat and uninspiring face in front of him he was inclined to resent it.

"What does your Majesty propose to do?" he asked shortly.

"I propose to do the following Upon you rests the chief burden."

The Chancellor did not look surprised.

"It will be your part to break the news as gently as possible to my people. You will begin by saying that I am busy with a great enchanter who has called to see me, and that therefore I am unable to show myself to my people this morning. Later on in the day you will announce that the enchanter has shown me how to defeat the wicked Euralians; you will dwell upon the fact that this victory, as assured by him, involves an overwhelming sacrifice on my part, but that for the good of my people I am willing to endure it. Then you will solemnly announce that the sacrifice I am making, have indeed already made, is nothing less than . . . What are all those fools cheering for out there?" A mighty roar of laughter rose to the sky. "Here, what's it all about? Just go and look."

The Chancellor went to the door of the tent—and saw.

He came back to the King, striving to speak casually.

"Just a humorous emblem that the Euralians have raised over their camp," he said. "It wouldn't amuse your Majesty."

"I am hardly in the mood for joking," said the King. "Let us return to business. As I was saying, you will announce to the people that the enormous sacrifice which their King is prepared to make for them consists of . . . There they go again. I must really see what it is. Just pull the door back so that I may see without being seen."

"It—it really wouldn't amuse your Majesty."

"Are you implying that I have no sense of humour?" said the King sternly.

"Oh no, sire, but there are certain jokes, jokes in the poorest of taste, that would naturally not appeal to so delicate a palate as your Majesty's. This—er—strikes me as one of them."

"Of that, I am the best judge," said the King coldly. "Open the door at once."

The Chancellor opened the door; and there before the King's eyes, flaunting themselves in the breeze beneath the Royal Standard of Euralia, waved his own beloved whiskers.

The King of Barodia was not a lovable man, and his daughters were decidedly plain, but there are moments when one cannot help admiring him. This was one of them.

"You may shut the door," he said to the Chancellor. "The instructions which I gave you just now," he went on in the same cold voice, "are cancelled. Let me think for a moment." He began to walk up and down his apartment. "You may think, too," he added kindly. "If you have anything not entirely senseless to suggest, you may suggest it."

He continued his pacings. Suddenly he came to a dead stop. He was standing in front of a large mirror. For the first time since he was seventeen he had seen his face without whiskers. His eyes still fixed on his reflection, he beckoned the Chancellor to approach.

"Come here," he said, clutching him by the arm. "You see that?" He pointed to the reflection. "That is what I look like? The mirror hasn't made a mistake of any kind? That is really and truly what I look like?"

"Yes, sire."

For a little while the King continued to gaze, fascinated, at his reflection, and then he turned on the Chancellor.

"You coward!" he said. "You weak-kneed, jelly-souled, paper-livered imitation of a man! You cringe to a King who looks like that! Why, you ought to *kick* me."

The Chancellor remembered that he had one

kick owing to him. He drew back his foot, and then a thought occurred to him.

"You might kick me back," he pointed out.

"I certainly should," said the King.

The Chancellor hesitated a moment.

"I think," he said, "that these private quarrels in the face of the common enemy are to be deplored."

The King looked at him, gave a short laugh, and went on walking up and down.

"That face again." He sighed as he came opposite the mirror. "No, it's no good; I can never be King like this. I shall abdicate."

"But, your Majesty, this is a very terrible decision. Could not your Majesty live in retirement until your Majesty had grown your Majesty's whiskers again? Surely this is—"

The King came to a stand opposite him and looked down on him gravely.

"Chancellor," he said, "those whiskers which you have just seen fluttering in the breeze have been for more than forty years my curse. For more than forty years I have had to live up to those whiskers, behaving, not as my temperament, which is a kindly, indeed a genial one, bade me behave, but as those whiskers insisted I should behave. Arrogant, hasty-tempered, overbearing—these are the qualities which have been demanded of the owner of those whiskers. I played a part which was difficult at first; of late, it has, alas! been more easy. Yet it has never been my true nature that you have seen."

He paused and looked silently at himself in the glass.

"But, your Majesty," said the Chancellor eagerly, "why choose this moment to abdicate? Think how your country will welcome this new King whom you have just revealed to me. And yet," he added regretfully, "it would not be quite the same."

The King turned round to him.

"There spoke a true Barodian," he said. "It would not be the same. Barodians have come to expect certain qualities from their rulers, and they would be lost without them. A new King might accustom them to other ways, but they are used to me, and they would not like me different. No, Chancellor, I shall abdicate. Do not wear so sad a face for me. I am looking forward to my new life with the greatest of joy."

The Chancellor was not looking sad for him; he was looking sad for himself, thinking that perhaps a new King might like changes in Chancellors equally with changes in manners or whiskers.

"But what will you do?" he asked.

"I shall be a simple subject of the new King, earning my living by my own toil."

The Chancellor raised his eyebrows at this.

"I suppose you think," said the King haughtily, "that I have not the intelligence to earn my own living."

The Chancellor, with a cough, remarked that the very distinguished qualities which made an excellent King did not always imply the corresponding—er—and so on.

"That shows how little you know about it. Just to give one example. I happen to know that I have in me the makings of an excellent swineherd."

"A swineherd?"

"The man who—er—herds the swine. It may surprise you to hear that, posing as a swineherd, I have conversed with another of the profession upon his own subject, without his suspecting the truth. It is just such a busy outdoor life as I should enjoy. One herds and one milks, and one milks, and—er—herds, and so it goes on, day after day." A happy smile, the first the Chancellor had ever seen there, spread itself over his features. He slapped the Chancellor playfully on the back and added, "I shall simply love it."

The Chancellor was amazed. What a story for his dinner parties when the war was over!

"How will you announce it?" he asked, and his tone struck a happy mean between the tones in which you address a monarch and a pig-minder respectively.

"That will be your duty. Now that I have shaken off the curse of those whiskers, I am no longer a proud man, but even a swineherd would not care for it to get about that he had been forcibly shaved while sleeping. That this should be the last incident recorded of me in Barodian history is unbearable. You will announce therefore that I have been slain in fair combat, though at dead of night, by the King of Euralia, and that my whiskers fly over his royal tent as a symbol of his victory." He winked at the Chancellor and added, "It might as well get about that someone had stolen my Magic Sword that evening."

The Chancellor was speechless with admiration and approval of the plan. Like his brother of Euralia, he, too, was longing to get home again. The war had arisen over a personal insult to the King. If the King was no longer King, why should the war go on?

"I think," said the future swineherd, "that I shall send a Note over to the King of Euralia, telling him my decision. Tonight, when it is dark, I shall steal away and begin my new life. There seems to be no reason why the people should not go back to their homes tomorrow. By the way, that guard outside there knows that I wasn't killed last night; that's rather awkward."

"I think," said the Chancellor, who was already picturing his return home and was not going to be done out of it by a common sentry, "I think I could persuade him that you *were* killed last night."

"Oh, well, then, that's all right." He drew a ring from his finger. "Perhaps this will help him to be persuaded. Now leave me while I write to the King of Euralia."

It was a letter which Merriwig was decidedly glad to get. It announced bluntly that the war was over, and added that the King of Barodia proposed to abdicate. His son would rule in his stead, but he was a harmless fool, and the King of Euralia need not bother about him. The King would be much obliged if he would let it get about that the whiskers had been won in fair fight; this would really be more to the credit of both of them. Personally, he was glad to be rid of the things, but one has one's dignity. He was now retiring into private life, and if it were rumoured abroad that he had been killed by the King of Euralia, matters would be much more easy to arrange.

Merriwig slept late after his long night abroad, and he found this Note waiting for him when he awoke. He summoned the Chancellor at once.

"What have you done about those—er—trophies?" he asked.

"They are fluttering from your flagstaff, sire, at this moment."

"Ah! And what do my people say?"

"They are roaring with laughter, sire, at the whimsical nature of the jest."

"Yes, but what do they say?"

"Some say that your Majesty, with great cunning, ventured privily in the night and cut them off while he slept; others, that with great bravery you defeated him in mortal combat and carried them away as the spoils of the victor."

"Oh! And what did *you* say?"

The Chancellor looked reproachful.

"Naturally, your Majesty, I have not spoken with them."

"Ah, well, I have been thinking it over in the night, and I remember now that I *did* kill him. You understand?"

"Your Majesty's skill in swordplay will be much appreciated by the people."

"Quite so," said the King hastily. "Well, that's all—I'm getting up now. And we're all going home tomorrow."

The Chancellor went out, rubbing his hands with delight.

18

The Veteran of the Forest Entertains Two Very Young People

DO YOU REMEMBER the day when the Princess Hyacinth and Wiggs sat upon the castle walls and talked of Udo's coming? The Princess thought he would be dark, and Wiggs thought he would be fair, and he was to have the Purple Room—or was it the Blues?—and anyhow he was to put the Countess in her place and bring happiness to Euralia. That seemed a long time ago to Hyacinth now, as once more she sat on the castle walls with Wiggs.

She was very lonely. She longed to get rid of that "outside help in our affairs" which she had summoned so recklessly. They were two against one now. Belvane actively against her was bad enough; but Belvane in the background with Udo as her mouthpiece—Udo specially asked in to give the benefit of his counsel—this was ten times worse.

"What do you do, Wiggs," she asked, "when you are very lonely and nobody loves you?"

"Dance," said Wiggs promptly.

"But if you don't want to dance?"

Wiggs tried to remember those dark ages (about a week ago) when she couldn't dance.

"I used to go into the forest," she said, "and sit under my own tree, and by and by everybody loved you."

"I wonder if they'd love *me*."

"Of course they would. Shall I show you my special tree?"

"Yes, but don't come with me; tell me where it is. I want to be unhappy alone."

So Wiggs told her how you followed her special path, which went in at the corner of the forest, until by and by the trees thinned on either side, and it widened into a glade, and you went downhill and crossed the brook at the bottom and went up the other side until it was all trees again, and the first and the biggest and the oldest and the loveliest was hers. And you turned round and sat with your back against it, and looked across to where you'd come from, and then you *knew* that everything was all right.

"I shall find it," said Hyacinth, as she got up. "Thank you, dear."

She found it, she sat there, and her heart was very bitter at first against Udo and against Belvane, and even against her father for going away and leaving her; but by and by the peace of the place wrapped itself round her, and she felt that she would find a way out of her difficulties somehow. Only she wished that her father would come back, because he loved her, and she felt that it would be nice to be loved again.

"It is beautiful, isn't it?" said a voice from behind her.

She turned suddenly as a tall young man stepped out from among the trees.

"Oh, who are you, please?" she asked, amazed at his sudden appearance. His dress told her nothing, but his face told her things which she was glad to know.

"My name," he said, "is Coronel."

"It is a pretty name."

"Yes, but don't be led away by it. It belongs to nobody very particular. Do you mind if I sit down? I generally sit down here about this time."

"Oh, do you live in the forest?"

"I have lived here for the last week." He gave her a friendly smile and added, "You're late, aren't you?"

"Late?"

"Yes, I've been expecting you for the last seven days."

"How did you know there was any me at all?" Hyacinth smiled.

With a movement of his hand Coronel indicated the scene in front of him.

"There had to be *somebody* for whom all this was made. It wanted somebody to say 'Thank you' to it now and then."

"Haven't you been doing that all this week?"

"Me? I wouldn't presume. No, it's your glade, and you've neglected it shamefully."

"There's a little girl who comes here," said Hyacinth. "I wonder if you have seen her?"

Coronel turned away. There were secret places in his heart into which Hyacinth could not come—yet.

"She danced," he said shortly.

There was silence between them for a little, but a comfortable silence, as if they were already old friends.

"You know," said Hyacinth, looking down at him as he lay at her feet, "you ought not to be here at all, really."

"I wish I could think that," said Coronel. "I had a horrible feeling that duty called me here. I love those places where one really oughtn't to be at all, don't you?"

"I love being here." Hyacinth sighed. "Wiggs was quite right." Seeing him look up at her, she added, "Wiggs is the little girl who dances, you know."

"She would be right," said Coronel, looking away from her.

Hyacinth felt strangely rested. It seemed that never again would anything trouble her; never again would she have only her own strength to depend upon. Who was he? But it did not matter. He might go away and she might never see him again, but she was no longer afraid of the world.

"I thought," she said, "that all the men of Euralia were away fighting."

"So did I," said Coronel.

"What are you, then? A Prince from a distant country, an enchanter, a spy sent from Barodia, a travelling musician?—you see, I give you much to choose from."

"You leave me nothing to be but what I am—Coronel."

"And I am Hyacinth."

He knew, of course, but he made no sign.

"Hyacinth," he said, and he held out his hand.

"Coronel," she answered as she took it.

The brook chuckled to itself as it hurried past below them.

Hyacinth got up with a little sigh of contentment.

"Well, I must be going," she said.

"Must you really be going?" asked Coronel. "I wasn't saying goodbye, you know."

"I really must."

"It's a surprising thing about the view from here," said Coronel, "that it looks just as nice tomorrow. Tomorrow about the same time."

"That's a very extraordinary thing." Hyacinth smiled.

"Yes, but it's one of those things that you don't want to take another person's word for."

"You think I ought to see for myself? Well, perhaps I will."

"Give me a whistle if I happen to be passing," said Coronel casually, "and tell me what you think. Goodbye, Hyacinth."

"Goodbye, Coronel."

She nodded her head confidently at him, and then turned round and went off daintily down the hill.

Coronel stared after her.

"What *is* Udo doing?" he murmured to himself. "But perhaps she doesn't like animals. A whole day to wait. How endless!"

If he had known that Udo, now on two legs again, was at that moment in Belvane's garden, trying to tell her, for the fifth time that week, about his early life in Araby, he would have been still more surprised.

We left Coronel, if you remember, in Araby. For three or four days he remained there, wondering how Udo was getting on, and feeling more and more that he ought to do something about it. On the fourth day he got on to his horse and rode off again. He simply must see what was happening. If Udo wanted help, then he would be there to give it; if Udo was all right again, then he could go comfortably back to Araby.

To tell the truth, Coronel was a little jealous of his friend. A certain Prince Perivale, who had stayed at his uncle's court, had once been a suitor for Hyacinth's hand; but losing a competition with the famous seven-headed bull of Euralia, which Merriwig had arranged for him, had made no further headway with his suit. This Prince had had a portrait of Hyacinth specially done for him by his own Court Painter, a portrait which Coronel had seen. It was for this reason that he had at first objected to accompanying Udo to Euralia, and it was for this reason that he persuaded himself very readily that the claims of friendship called him there now.

For the last week he had been waiting in the forest. Now that he was there, he was not quite sure how to carry out his mission. So far there had been no sign of Udo, either on four legs or on two; it seemed probable that unless Coronel went to the Palace and asked for him, there would be no sign. And if he went to the Palace, and Udo was all right and the Princess Hyacinth was in love with him, then the worst would have happened. He would have to stay there and help admire Udo—an unsatisfying prospect to a man in love. For he told himself by this time that he was in love with Hyacinth, although he had never seen her.

So he had waited in the forest, hoping for something to turn up; and first Wiggs had come . . . and now at last Hyacinth. He was very glad that he had waited.

She was there on the morrow.

"I knew you'd come," said Coronel. "It looks just as beautiful, doesn't it?"

"I think it's even more beautiful," said Hyacinth.

"You mean those little white clouds? That was my idea, putting those in. I thought you'd like them."

"I wondered what you did all day. Does it keep you very busy?"

"Oh," said Coronel, "I have time for singing."

"Why do you sing?"

"Because I am young and the forest is beautiful."

"I have been singing this morning, too."

"Why?" asked Coronel eagerly.

"Because the war with Barodia is over."

"Oh!" said Coronel, rather taken aback.

"That doesn't interest you. Yet if you were a Euralian—"

"But it interests me extremely. Let us admire the scene for a moment, while I think. Look, there is another of my little clouds."

Coronel wondered what would happen now. If the King were coming back, then Udo would be wanted no longer save as a suitor for Hyacinth's hand. If, then, he returned, it would show that . . . But suppose he was still an animal? It was doubtful if he would go back to Araby as an animal. And then there was another possibility: perhaps he had never come to Euralia at all. Here were a lot of questions to be answered, and here next to him was one who could answer them. But he must go carefully.

"Ninety-seven, ninety-eight, ninety-nine, a hundred," he said aloud. "There, I've finished my thinking and you've finished your looking."

"And what have you decided?" Hyacinth smiled.

"Decided?" said Coronel, rather startled. "Oh, no, I wasn't deciding anything, I was just thinking. I was thinking about animals."

"So was I."

"How very curious, and also how wrong of you. You were supposed to be admiring my clouds. What sort of animals were you thinking about?"

"Oh—all sorts."

"I was thinking about rabbits. Do you care for rabbits at all?"

"Not very much."

"Neither do I. They're so loppity. Do you like lions?"

"I think their tails are rather silly," said Hyacinth.

"Yes, perhaps they are. Now—a woolly lamb."

"I am not very fond of woolly lambs just now."

"No? Well, they're not very interesting. It's a funny thing," he went on casually, trying to steal a glance at her, "that we should be talking about those three animals, because I once met somebody who was a mixture of all three together at the same time."

"So did I," said Hyacinth gravely.

But he saw her mouth trembling, and suddenly she turned round and caught his eye, and then they burst out laughing together.

"Poor Udo," said Coronel; "and how is he looking now?"

"He is all right again now."

"All right again? Then why isn't he . . . But I'm very glad he isn't."

"I didn't like him," said Hyacinth, blushing a little. And then she went on bravely, "But I think he found he didn't like me first."

"He wants humouring," said Coronel. "It's my business to humour him, it isn't yours."

Hyacinth looked at him with a new interest.

"Now I know who you are," she said. "He talked about you once."

"What did he say?" asked Coronel, obviously dying to know.

"He said that you were good at poetry."

Coronel was a little disappointed. He would have preferred Hyacinth to have been told that he was good at dragons. However, they had met now, and it did not matter.

"Princess," he said suddenly, "I expect you wonder what I am doing here. I came to see if Prince Udo was in need of help, and also to see if you were in need of help. Prince Udo was my friend, but if he has not been a friend of yours, then he is no longer a friend of mine. Tell me what has been happening here, and then tell me if in any way I can help you."

"You called me Hyacinth yesterday," she said, "and it is still my name."

"Hyacinth," said Coronel, taking her hand, "tell me if you want me at all."

"Thank you, Coronel. You see, Coronel, it's like this." And sitting beneath Wiggs's veteran of the forest, with Coronel lying at her feet, she told him everything.

"It seems easy enough," he said when she had finished. "You want Udo pushed out and the Countess put in her place. I can do the one while you do the other."

"Yes, but how do I push Prince Udo out?"

"That's what I*m* going to do."

"Yes, but, Coronel dear, if I could put the Countess in her place, shouldn't I have done it a long time ago? I don't think you quite know the sort of person she is. And I don't quite know what her place is either, which makes it rather hard to put her into it. You see, I don't think I told you that—that Father is rather fond of her."

"I thought you said Udo was."

"They both are."

"Then how simple. We simply kill Udo, and—and—well, anyhow, there's one part of it done."

"Yes, but what about the other part?"

Coronel thought for a moment.

"Would it be simpler if we did it the other way round?" he said. "Killed the Countess and put Udo in his place."

"Father wouldn't like that at all, and he's coming back tomorrow."

Coronel didn't quite see the difficulty. If the King was in love with the Countess, he would marry her whatever Hyacinth did. And what was the good of putting her in her place for one day if her next place was to be on the throne.

Hyacinth guessed what he was thinking.

"Oh, don't you see," she cried, "she doesn't know that the King is coming back tomorrow. And if I can only just show her—I don't mind if it's only for an hour—that I am not afraid of her, and that she has got to take her orders from me, then I shan't mind so much all that has happened these last weeks. But if she is to have disregarded me all the time, if she is to have plotted against me from the very moment my father went away, and if nothing is to come to her for it but that she marries my father and becomes Queen of Euralia, then I can have no pride left, and I will be a Princess no longer."

"I must see this Belvane," said Coronel thoughtfully.

"Oh, Coronel, Coronel," cried Hyacinth, "if *you* fall in love with her, too, I think I shall die of shame!"

"With *her*, Hyacinth?" he said, turning to her in amazement.

"Yes, you—I didn't—you never—I . . ." Her voice trailed away; she could not meet his gaze any longer; she dropped her eyes, and the next moment his arms were round her, and she knew that she would never be alone again.

19
Udo Behaves Like a Gentleman

"AND NOW," SAID Coronel, "we'd better decide what to do."

"But I don't mind what we do now," said Hyacinth happily. "She may have the throne and Father and Udo, and—and anything else she can get, and I shan't mind a bit. You see, I have got *you* now, Coronel, and I can never be jealous of anybody again."

"That's what makes it so jolly. We can do what we like, and it doesn't matter if it doesn't come off. So just for fun, let's think of something to pay her out."

"I feel I don't want to hurt anybody today."

"All right, we won't hurt her, we'll humour her. We will be her most humble obedient servants. She shall have everything she wants."

"Including Prince Udo." Hyacinth smiled.

"That's a splendid idea. We'll make her have

Udo. It will annoy your father, but one can't please everybody. Oh, I can see myself enjoying this."

They got up and wandered back along Wiggs's path, hand in hand.

"I'm almost afraid to leave the forest," said Hyacinth, "in case something happens."

"What should happen?"

"I don't know; but all our life together has been in the forest, and I'm just a little afraid of the world."

"I will be very close to you always, Hyacinth."

"Be very close, Coronel," she whispered, and then they walked out together.

If any of the servants at the Palace were surprised to see Coronel, they did not show it. After all, that was their business.

"Prince Coronel will be staying here," said the Princess. "Prepare a room for him and some refreshment for us both." And if they discussed those things in the servants' halls of those days (as why should they not?), no doubt they told each other that the Princess Hyacinth (bless her pretty face!) had found her man at last. Why, you only had to see her looking at him. But I get no assistance from Roger at this point; he pretends that he has a mind far above the gossip of the lower orders.

"I say," said Coronel as they went up the grand staircase, "I'm not a Prince, you know. Don't say I have deceived you."

"You are *my* Prince," said Hyacinth proudly.

"My dear, I am a king among men today, and you are my queen, but that's in our own special country of two."

"If you are so particular," said Hyacinth, with a smile, "Father will make you a proper Prince directly he comes back."

"Will he? That's what I'm wondering. You see he doesn't know yet about our little present to the Countess."

But it is quite time we got back to Belvane; we have left her alone too long. It was more than Udo did. Just now he was with her in her garden, telling her for the fifth time an extraordinarily dull story about an encounter of his with a dragon, apparently in its dotage, to which Belvane was listening with an interest which surprised even the narrator.

"And then," said Udo, "I jumped quickly to the right, and whirling my—no, wait a bit, that was later—I jumped quickly to my left—yes, I remember it now, it *was* my left—I jumped quickly to my left, and whirling my . . ."

He stopped suddenly at the expression on Belvane's face. She was looking over his shoulder at something behind him.

"Why, whoever is this?" she said, getting to her feet.

Before Udo had completely cleared his mind

of his dragon, the Princess and Coronel were upon them.

"Ah, Countess, I thought we should find you together," said Hyacinth archly. "Let me present to you my friend, the Duke Coronel. Coronel, this is Countess Belvane, a very dear and faithful friend of mine. Prince Udo, of course, you know. His Royal Highness and the Countess are—well, it isn't generally known at present, so perhaps I oughtn't to say anything."

Coronel made a deep bow to the astonished Belvane.

"Your humble servant," he said. "You will, I am sure, forgive me if I say how glad I am to hear your news. Udo is one of my oldest friends"—he turned and clapped that bewildered Highness on the back—"aren't you, Udo? and I can think of no one more suitable in every way." He bowed again, and turned back to the Prince. "Well, Udo, you're looking splendid. A different thing, Countess, from when I last saw him. Let me see, that must have been just the day before he arrived in Euralia. Ah, what a miracle-worker True Love is!"

I think one of the things which made Belvane so remarkable was that she was never afraid of remaining silent when she was not quite sure what to say. She waited therefore while she considered what all this meant; who Coronel was, what he was doing there, even whether a marriage with Udo was not after all the best that she could hope for now.

Meanwhile Udo, of course, blundered along gaily.

"We aren't exactly, Princess—I mean . . . What are you doing here, Coronel?—I didn't know, Princess, that you . . . The Countess and I were just having a little—I was just telling her what you said about . . . How did you get here, Coronel?"

"Shall we tell him?" said Coronel, with a smile at Hyacinth.

Hyacinth nodded.

"I rode," said Coronel. "It's a secret," he added.

"But I didn't know that you—"

"We find that we have really known each other a very long time," explained Hyacinth.

"And hearing that there was to be a wedding . . ." added Coronel.

Belvane made up her mind. Coronel was evidently a very different man from Udo. If he stayed in Euralia as adviser—more than adviser she guessed—to Hyacinth, her own position would not be in much doubt. And as for the King, it might be months before he came back, and when he did come, would he remember her? But to be Queen of Araby was no mean thing.

"We didn't want it to be known yet," she

said shyly, "but you have guessed our secret, your Royal Highness." She looked modestly at the ground, and, feeling for her reluctant lover's hand, went on, "Udo and I"—here she squeezed the hand, and, finding it was Coronel's, took Udo's boldly without any more maidenly nonsense—"Udo and I love each other."

"Say something, Udo," prompted Coronel.

"Er—yes," said Udo, very unwillingly, and deciding that he would explain it all afterwards. Whatever his feelings for the Countess, he was not going to be rushed into a marriage.

"Oh, I'm so glad," said Hyacinth. "I felt somehow that it must be coming, because you've seen so *much* of each other lately. Wiggs and I have often talked about it together."

(What has happened to the child? thought Belvane. She isn't a child at all, she's grown up.)

"There's no holding Udo once he begins," volunteered Coronel. "He's the most desperate lover in Araby."

"My father will be so excited when he hears," said Hyacinth. "You know, of course, that his Majesty comes back tomorrow with all his army."

She did not swoon nor utter a cry. She did not plead the vapours or the megrims. She took, unflinching, what must have been the biggest shock in her life.

"Then perhaps I had better see that everything is ready in the Palace," she said, "if your Royal Highness will excuse me." And with a curtsy she was gone.

Coronel exchanged a glance with Hyacinth. "I'm enjoying this," he seemed to say.

"Well," she announced, "I must be going in, too. There'll be much to see about."

Coronel was left alone with the most desperate lover in Araby.

"And now," said the Prince, "tell me what you are doing here."

Coronel put his arm in Udo's and walked him up and down the flagged path.

"Your approaching marriage," he said, "is the talk of Araby. Naturally, I had to come here to see for myself what she was like. My dear Udo, she's charming; I congratulate you."

"Don't be a fool, Coronel. I haven't the slightest intention of marrying her."

"Then why have you told everybody that you are going to?"

"You know quite well I haven't told anybody. There hasn't been a single word about it mentioned until you pushed your way in just now."

"Ah, well, perhaps you hadn't heard about it. But the Princess knows, the Countess knows, and I know—yes, I think you may take our word for it that it's true."

"I haven't the slightest intention—what do you keep clinging on to my arm like this for?"

"My dear Udo, I'm so delighted to see you again. Don't turn your back on old friendships just because you have found a nobler and a truer . . . Oh, very well, if you're going to drop all your former friends, go on then. But when *I'm* married, there will always be a place for—"

"Understand once and for all," said Udo angrily, "that I am *not* getting married. No, don't take my arm—we can talk quite well like this."

"I am sorry, Udo," said Coronel meekly; "we seem to have made a mistake. But you must admit we found you in a very compromising position."

"It wasn't in the least compromising," protested Udo indignantly. "As a matter of fact, I was just telling her about that dragon I killed in Araby last year."

"Ah, and who would listen to a hopeless story like that, but the woman one was going to marry?"

"Once more, I am not going to marry her."

"Well, you must please yourself, but you have compromised her severely with that story. Poor innocent girl. Well, let's forget about it. And now tell me, how do you like Euralia?"

"I am returning to Araby this afternoon," said Udo stiffly.

"Well, perhaps you're right. I hope that nothing will happen to you on the way."

Udo, who was about to enter the Palace, turned round with a startled look.

"What do you mean?"

"Well, something happened on the way here. By the by, how did that happen? You never told me."

"Your precious Countess, whom you expect me to marry."

"How very unkind of her. A nasty person to annoy." He was silent for a moment, and then added thoughtfully, "I suppose it *is* rather annoying to think you're going to marry somebody whom you love very much, and then find you're not going to."

Udo evidently hadn't thought of this. He tried to show that he was not in the least frightened.

"She couldn't do anything. It was only by a lucky chance she did it last time."

"Yes, but of course the chance might come again. You'd have the thing hanging over you always. She's clever, you know; and I should never feel quite safe if she were my enemy. . . . Lovely flowers, aren't they? What's the name of this one?"

Udo dropped undecidedly into a seat. This wanted thinking out. The Countess—what was wrong with her, after all? And she evidently adored him. Of course that was not surprising; the question was, was it fair to disappoint one who had, perhaps, some little grounds for . . . After all, he had been no more gallant than was customary from a Prince and a gentleman to a beautiful woman. It was her own fault if she had mistaken his intentions. Of course he ought to have left Euralia long ago. But he had stayed on, and—well, decidedly she was beautiful—perhaps he had paid rather too much attention to that. And he had certainly neglected the Princess a little. After all, again, why not marry the Countess? It was absurd to suppose there was anything in Coronel's nonsense, but one never knew. Not that he was marrying her out of fear. No; certainly not. It was simply a chivalrous whim on his part. The poor woman had misunderstood him, and she should not be disappointed.

"She seems fond of flowers," said Coronel. "You ought to make the Palace garden look beautiful between you."

"Now, understand clearly, Coronel, I'm not in the least frightened by the Countess."

"My dear Udo, what a speech for a lover! Of course you're not. After all, what you bore with such patience and dignity once, you can bear again."

"That subject is distasteful to me. I must ask you not to refer to it. If I marry the Countess—"

"You'll be a very lucky man," put in Coronel. "I happen to know that the King of Euralia—however, she's chosen you, it seems. Personally, I can't make out what she sees in you. What is it?"

"I should have thought it was quite obvious," said Udo with dignity. "Well, Coronel, I think perhaps you are right and that it's my duty to marry her."

Coronel shook him solemnly by the hand.

"I congratulate your Royal Highness. I will announce your decision to the Princess. She will be much amu—much delighted." And he turned into the Palace.

Pity him, you lovers. He had not seen Hyacinth for nearly ten minutes.

20

Coronel Knows a Good Story When He Hears It

I QUOTE (with slight alterations) from an epic by Charlotte Patacake, a contemporary poet of the country:

"King Merriwig the First rode back from war,
   As many other Kings had done before;
   Five hundred men behind him were in sight
(Left-right, left-right, left-right, left-right,
   left-right)."

So far as is known, this was her only work, but she built up some reputation on it, and Belvane, who was a good judge, had a high opinion of her genius.

To be exact, there were only four hundred and ninety-nine men. Henry Smallnose, a bowman of considerable promise, had been left behind in the enemy's country, the one casualty of the war. While spying out the land in the early days of the invasion, he had been discovered by the Chief Armourer of Barodia at full length on the wet grass searching for tracks. The Chief Armourer, a kindly man, had invited him to his cottage, dried him, and given him a warming drink, and had told him that, if ever his spying took him that way again, he was not to stand on ceremony, but come in and pay him a visit. Henry, having caught a glimpse of the Chief Armourer's daughter, had accepted without any false pride, and had frequently dropped in to supper thereafter. Now that the war was over, he found that he could not tear himself away. With King Merriwig's permission, he was settling in Barodia, and with the Chief Armourer's permission, he was starting on his new life as a married man.

As the towers of the castle came in sight, Merriwig drew a deep breath of happiness. Home again! The hardships of the war were over; the spoils of victory (wrapped up in tissue paper) were in his pocket; days of honoured leisure were waiting for him. He gazed at each remembered landmark of his own beloved country, his heart overflowing with thankfulness. Never again would he leave Euralia!

How good to see Hyacinth again! Poor little Hyacinth left all alone; but there! she had had the Countess Belvane, a woman of great experience, to help her. Belvane! Should he risk it? How much had she thought of him while he was away? Hyacinth would be growing up and getting married soon. Life would be lonely in Euralia then, unless . . . Should he risk it?

What would Hyacinth say?

She was waiting for him at the gates of the castle. She had wanted Coronel to wait with her, but he had refused.

"We must offer the good news to him gradually," he said. "When a man has just come back from a successful campaign, he doesn't want to find a surprise like this waiting for him. Just think—we don't even know why the war is over—he must be longing to tell you that. Oh, he'll have a hundred things to tell you first; but then, when he says 'And what's been happening here while I've been away? Nothing much, I suppose?' then you can say—"

"Then I shall say, 'Nothing much; only Coronel.' And such a clever!"

"Oh, I have my ideas," said Coronel. "Well, I'll be out of the way somewhere. I think I'll go for a walk in the forest. Or shall I stay here, in the Countess's garden, and amuse myself with Udo? Anyhow, I'll give you an hour alone together first."

The cavalcade drew up in front of the castle. Handkerchiefs fluttered to them from the walls; trumpets were blown; hounds bayed. Down the steps came Hyacinth, all blue and gold, and flung herself into her father's arms.

"My dear child," said Merriwig as he patted her soothingly. "There, there! It's your old father come back again. H'r'm. There, there!" He patted her again, as though it were she and not himself who was in danger of breaking down. "My little Hyacinth! My own little girl!"

"Oh, Father, I *am* glad to have you back."

"There, there, my child. Now I must just say a few words to my men, and then we can tell each other all that has been happening."

He took a step forward and addressed his troops.

"Men of Euralia (*cheers*). We have returned from a long and arduous conflict (*cheers*) to the embraces (*loud cheers*) of our mothers and wives and daughters (*prolonged cheering*)—as the case may be (*hear, hear*). In honour of our great victory I decree that, from now onward, tomorrow shall be observed as a holiday throughout Euralia (*terrific cheering*). I bid you all now return to your homes, and I hope that you will find as warm a welcome there as I have found in mine." Here he turned and embraced his daughter again, and if his eye travelled over her shoulder in the direction of Belvane's garden, it is a small matter, and one for which the architect of the castle, no doubt, was principally to blame.

There was another storm of cheers, the battle

cry of Euralia, *"Ho, ho, Merriwig!"* was shouted from five hundred throats, and the men dispersed happily to their homes. Hyacinth and Merriwig went into the Palace.

"Now, Father," said Hyacinth later on, when Merriwig had changed his clothes and refreshed himself, "you've got to tell me all about it. I can hardly believe it's really over."

"Yes, yes. It's all over," said Merriwig heartily. "We shan't have any trouble in *that* direction again, I fancy."

"Do tell me, did the King of Barodia apologize?"

"He did better than that, he abdicated."

"Why?"

"Well," said Merriwig, remembering just in time, "I—er—killed him."

"Oh, Father, how rough of you."

"I don't think it hurt him very much, my dear. It was more a shock to his feelings than anything else. See, I have brought these home for you."

He produced from his pocket a small packet in tissue paper.

"Oh, how exciting! Whatever can it be?"

Merriwig unwrapped the paper, and disclosed a couple of ginger whiskers, neatly tied up with blue ribbon.

"Father!"

He picked out the left one, *fons et origo* (if he

had known any Latin) of the war, and held it up for Hyacinth's inspection.

"There, you can see the place where Henry Smallnose's arrow bent it. By the way," he added, "Henry is marrying, and settling down in Barodia. It is curious," he went on, "how after a war one's thoughts turn to matrimony." He glanced at his daughter to see how she would take this, but she was still engrossed with the whiskers.

"What am I going to do with them, Father? I can't plant them in the garden."

"I thought we might run them up the flag-staff, as we did in Barodia."

"Isn't that a little unkind now that the poor man's dead?"

Merriwig looked round him to see that there were no eavesdroppers.

"Can you keep a secret?" he asked mysteriously.

"Of course," said Hyacinth, deciding at once that it would not matter if she only told Coronel.

"Well, then, listen."

He told her of his secret journey to the King of Barodia's tent; he told her of the King of Barodia's letter; he told her more fully of his early duel with the King; he told her everything that he had said and done; and everything that everybody else had said and done to him; and his boyish pleasure in it all was so evident and so innocent that even a stranger would have had nothing more reproachful for him than a smile. To Hyacinth he seemed the dearest of fathers and the most wonderful of kings.

And by and by the moment came of which Coronel had spoken.

"And now," said Merriwig, "tell me what you have all been doing with yourselves here. Nothing much, I suppose?"

He waited nervously, wondering if Hyacinth would realize that *all* was meant to include more particularly Belvane.

Hyacinth drew a stool up to her father's chair and sat down very close to him.

"Father," she said, stroking his hand where it rested on his knee, "I *have* got some news for you."

"Nothing about the Coun—nothing serious, I hope," said Merriwig, in alarm.

"It's rather serious, but it's rather nice. Father, dear, would you mind *very* much if I got married soon?"

"My dear, you shall get married as soon as you like. Let me see, there were six or seven Princes who came about it only the other day. I sent them off on adventures of some kind, but— dear me, yes, they ought to have been back by now. I suppose you haven't heard anything of them?"

"No, Father," said Hyacinth, with a little smile.

"Ah, well, no doubt they were unsuccessful. No matter, dear, we can easily find you plenty more suitors. Indeed, the subject has been very near my thoughts lately. We'll arrange a little competition, and let them know in the neighbouring countries; there'll be no lack of candidates. Let me see, there's that seven-headed bull; he's getting a little old now, but he was good enough for the last one. We might—"

"I don't want a suitor," said Hyacinth softly. "I have one."

Merriwig leaned forward with eagerness.

"My dear, this is indeed news. Tell me all about it. Upon what quest did you send him?"

Hyacinth had felt this coming. Had she lived in modern times, she would have expected the question, "What is his income?" A man must prove his worth in some way.

"I haven't sent him away at all yet," she said; "he's only just come. He's been very kind to me, and I'm sure you'll love him."

"Well, well, we'll arrange something for him. Perhaps that bull I was speaking of. . . . By the way, who is he?"

"He comes from Araby, and his name is—"

"Udo, of course. Why didn't I think of him? An excellent arrangement, my dear."

"It isn't Udo, I'm afraid, Father. It's Coronel."

"And who might Coronel be?" said the King, rather sternly.

"He's—he's—well, he's . . . Here he is, Father." She ran up to him impulsively as he came in at the door. "Oh, Coronel, you're just in time; do tell Father who you are."

Coronel bowed profoundly to the King.

"Before I explain myself, your Majesty," he said, "may I congratulate your Majesty on your wonderful victory over the Barodians? From the little I have gathered outside, it is the most remarkable victory that has ever occurred. But of course I am longing to hear the full story from your Majesty's own lips. Is it a fact that your Majesty made his way at dead of night to the King of Barodia's own tent and challenged him to mortal combat and slew him?" There was an eagerness, very winning, in his eyes as he asked it; he seemed to be envying the King such an adventure—an adventure after his own heart.

Merriwig was in an awkward position. He wondered for a moment whether to order his daughter out of the room. "Leave us, my child," he would say. "These are matters for men to discuss." But Hyacinth would know quite well why she had been sent out, and would certainly tell Coronel the truth of the matter afterwards.

It really looked as if Coronel would have to be let into the secret, too. He cleared his throat noisily by way of preparation.

"There are certain state reasons," he said with dignity, "why that story has been allowed to get about."

"Pardon, your Majesty. I have no wish to—"

"But as you know so much, you may as well know all. It happened like this." Once more he told the story of his midnight visit, and of the King's letter to him.

"But, your Majesty," cried Coronel, "it is more wonderful than the other. Never was such genius of invention, such brilliance and daring of execution."

"So you like it," said Merriwig, trying to look modest.

"I love it."

"I knew he'd love it," put in Hyacinth. "It's just the sort of story that Coronel would love. Tell him about how you fought the King at the beginning of the war, and how you pretended to be a swineherd, and how . . ."

Could any father have resisted? In a little while Hyacinth and Coronel were seated eagerly at his feet, and he was telling once more the great story of his adventures.

"Well, well," said the King at the end of it, when he had received their tribute of admiration. "Those are just a few of the little adventures that happen in wartime." He turned to Coronel. "And so you, I understand, wish to marry my daughter?"

"Does that surprise your Majesty?"

"Well, no, it doesn't. And she, I understand, wishes to marry you."

"Yes, please, Father."

"That," said Coronel simply, "is much more surprising."

Merriwig, however, was not so sure of that. He liked the look of Coronel, he liked his manner, and he saw at once that he knew a good story—when he heard one.

"Of course," he said, "you'll have to win her."

"Anything your Majesty sets me to do. It's as well," he added with a disarming smile, "that you cannot ask for the whiskers of the King of Barodia. There is only one man who could have got those."

Truly an excellent young man.

"Well, we'll arrange something," said Merriwig, looking pleased. "Perhaps your Prince Udo would care to be a competitor, too."

Hyacinth and Coronel interchanged a smile.

"Alas, Father," she said, "his Royal Highness is not attracted by my poor charms."

"Wait till he has seen them, my dear," said Merriwig with a chuckle.

"He has seen them, Father."

"What? You invited him here? Tell me about this, Hyacinth. He came to stay with you and he never—"

"His Royal Highness," put in Coronel, "has given his affections to another."

"Aha! So that's the secret. Now I wonder if I can guess who she is. What do you say to the Princess Elvira of Tregong? I know his father had hopes in that direction."

Hyacinth looked round at Coronel as if appealing for his support. He took a step toward her.

"No, it's not the Princess Elvira," said Hyacinth, a little nervously.

The King laughed good-humouredly.

"Ah, well, you must tell me," he said.

Hyacinth put out her hand, and Coronel pressed it encouragingly.

"His Royal Highness Prince Udo," she said, "is marrying the Countess Belvane."

21

A Serpent Coming after Udo

BELVANE HAD NOW had twenty-four hours in which to think it over.

Whatever her faults, she had a sense of humour. She could not help smiling to herself as she thought of that scene in the garden. However much she regretted her too hasty engagement, she was sure Udo regretted it still more. If she gave him the least opportunity, he would draw back from it.

Then why not give him the opportunity? "My dear Prince Udo, I'm afraid I mistook the nature of my feelings"—said, of course, with downcast head and a maidenly blush. Exit Udo with haste, enter King Merriwig. It would be so easy.

Ah, but then Hyacinth would have won. Hyacinth had forced the engagement upon her; even if it only lasted for twenty-four hours, so long as it was a forced engagement, Hyacinth would have had the better of her for that time. But if she welcomed the engagement, if she managed in some way to turn it to account, to make it appear as if she had wanted it all the time, then Hyacinth's victory would be no victory at all, but a defeat.

Marry Udo, then, as if willingly? Yes, but that was too high a price to pay. She was by this time thoroughly weary of him, and besides, she had every intention of marrying the King of Euralia. To pretend to marry him until she brought the King in open conflict with him, and then having led the King to her feet to dismiss the rival who had served her turn—that was her only wise course.

She did not come to this conclusion without much thought. She composed an Ode to Despair, an Elegy to an Unhappy Woman, and a Triolet to Interfering Dukes before her mind was made up. She also considered very seriously what she would look like in a little cottage in the middle of the forest, dressed in a melancholy grey and holding communion only with the birds and trees; a life of retirement away from the vain world; a life into which no man came. It had its attractions, but she decided that grey did not suit her.

She went down to her garden and sent for Prince Udo. At about the moment when the King was having the terrible news broken to him, Udo was protesting over the sundial that he loved Belvane and Belvane only, and that he was looking forward eagerly to the day when she would make him the happiest of men. So afraid was he of what might happen to him on the way back to Araby.

"The Countess Belvane!" cried Merriwig. "Prince Udo marry the Countess Belvane! I never heard of such a thing in my life." He glared at them one after the other as if it were their fault—as indeed it was. "Why didn't you tell me this before, Hyacinth?"

"It has only just been announced, Father."

"Who announced it?"

They looked across at each other.

"Well—er—Udo did," said Coronel.

"I never heard of anything so ridiculous in my life! I won't have it!"

"But, Father, don't you think she'd make a very good Queen?"

"She'd make a wonderful—that has nothing to do with it. What I feel so strongly about it is this. For month after month I am fighting in a strange country. After extraordinary scenes of violence and—peril—I come back to my own home to enjoy the—er—fruits of victory. No sooner do I get inside my door than I have all this thrust upon me."

"All what, Father?" said Hyacinth innocently.

"All *this*," said the King, with a circular movement of the hand. "It's too bad; upon my word it is. I won't have it. Now mind, Hyacinth, I *won't* have it."

"But, Father, how can I help it?"

Merriwig paid no attention to her.

"I come home," he went on indignantly, "fresh from the—er—spoils of victory to what I thought was my own peaceful—er—home. And what do I find? Somebody here wants to marry somebody there, and somebody else over there wants to marry somebody else over here; it's impossible to mention any person's name, in even the most casual way, without being told they are going to get married, or some nonsense of that sort. I'm very much upset about it."

"Oh, Father!" said Hyacinth penitently. "Won't you see the Countess yourself and talk to her?"

"To think that for weeks I have been looking forward to my return home and that now I should be met with this! It has quite spoiled my day."

"Father!" cried Hyacinth, coming toward him with outstretched hands.

"Let me send for her ladyship," began Coronel; "perhaps she— "

"No, no," said Merriwig, waving them away. "I am very much displeased with you both. What I have to do, I can do quite well by myself."

He strode out and slammed the door behind him.

Hyacinth and Coronel looked at each other blankly.

"My dear," said Coronel, "you never told me he was as fond of her as that."

"But I had no idea! Coronel, what can we do about it? Oh, I want him to marry her now. He's quite right—she'll make a wonderful Queen. Oh, my dear, I feel I want everybody to be as happy as we're going to be."

"They can't be that, but we'll do our best for them. I can manage Udo all right. I only have to say 'rabbits' to him, and he'll do anything for me. Hyacinth, I don't believe I've ever kissed you in this room yet, have I? Let's begin now."

Merriwig came upon the other pair of lovers in Belvane's garden. They were sharing a seat there, and Udo was assuring the Countess that he was her own little Udo-Wudo, and that they must never be away from each other again. The King put his hand in front of his eyes for a moment as if he could hardly bear it.

"Why, it's his Majesty," said Belvane, jumping up. She gave him a deep curtsy and threw in a bewitching smile on the top of it; formality or friendliness, he could take his choice. "Prince Udo of Araby, your Majesty." She looked shyly at him and added, "Perhaps you have heard."

"I have," said the King gloomily. "How do you do," he added in a melancholy voice.

Udo declared that he was in excellent health

at present, and would have gone into particulars about it, had not the King interrupted.

"Well, Countess," he said, "this is strange news to come back to. Shall I disturb you if I sit down with you for a little?"

"Oh, your Majesty, you would honour us. Udo, dear, have you seen the heronry lately?"

"Yes," said Udo.

"It looks so sweet just about this time of the afternoon."

"It does," said Udo.

Belvane gave a little shrug and turned to the King.

"I'm so longing to hear all your adventures," she murmured confidingly. "I got all your messages; it was so good of you to remember me."

"Ah," said Merriwig reproachfully, "and what do I find when I come back? I find . . ." He broke off, and indicated in pantomime with his eyebrows that he could explain better what he had found if Udo were absent.

"Udo, dear," said Belvane, turning to him, "have you seen the kennels lately?"

"Yes," said Udo.

"They look rather sweet just about this time," said Merriwig.

"Don't they?" said Udo.

"But I am so longing to hear," said Belvane, "how your Majesty defeated the King of Barodia. Was it your Majesty's wonderful spell which overcame the enemy?"

"You remember that?"

"Remember it? Oh, your Majesty! 'Bo boll . . .' Udo, dear, wouldn't you like to see the armoury?"

"No," said Udo.

"There are a lot of new things in it that I brought back from Barodia," said Merriwig hopefully.

"A lot of new things," explained Belvane.

"I'll see them later on," said Udo. "I dare say they'd look better in the evening."

"Then you shall show *me*, your Majesty," said Belvane. "Udo, dear, you can wait for me here."

The two of them moved off down the path together (Udo taken by surprise), and as soon as they were out of sight, tiptoed across the lawn to another garden seat, Belvane leading the way with her finger to her lips, and Merriwig following with an exaggerated caution which even Henry Smallnose would have thought overdone.

"He is a little slow, isn't he, that young man?" said the King as they sat down together. "I mean he didn't seem to understand—"

"He's such a devoted lover, your Majesty. He can't bear to be out of my sight for a moment."

"Oh, Belvane, this is a sad homecoming. For month after month I have been fighting and toiling, and planning and plotting and then . . .

Oh, Belvane, we were all so happy together before the war."

Belvane remembered that once she and the Princess and Wiggs had been so happy together, and that Udo's arrival had threatened to upset it all. One way and another, Udo had been a disturbing element in Euralia. But it would not do to let him go just yet.

"Aren't we still happy together?" she asked innocently. "There's her Royal Highness with her young Duke, and I have my dear Udo, and your Majesty has the—the Lord Chancellor—and all your Majesty's faithful subjects."

His Majesty gave a deep sigh.

"I am a very lonely man, Belvane. When Hyacinth leaves me, I shall have nobody left."

Belvane decided to risk it.

"Your Majesty should marry again," she said gently.

He looked unutterable things at her. He opened his mouth with the intention of doing his best to utter some of them, when . . .

"Not before Udo," said Belvane softly.

Merriwig got up indignantly and scowled at the Prince as the latter hurried over the lawn toward them.

"Well, really," said Merriwig, "I never knew such a place. One simply can't . . . Ah, your Royal Highness, have you seen our armoury? I should say," he corrected himself as he caught Belvane's reproachful look, "have *we* seen our armoury? We have. Her ladyship was much interested."

"I have no doubt, your Majesty." He turned to Belvane. "You will be interested in our armoury at home, dear."

She gave a quick glance at the King to see that he was looking, and then patted Udo's hand tenderly.

"Home," she said lovingly, "how sweet it sounds!"

The King shivered as if in pain, and strode quickly from them.

"Your Majesty sent for me," said Coronel.

The King stopped his pacings and looked round as Coronel came into the library.

"Ah, yes, yes," he said quickly. "Now sit down there and make yourself comfortable. I want to talk to you about this marriage."

"Which one, your Majesty?"

"Which one? Why, of course, yours—that is to say, Belvane's—or—rather . . ." He came to a stop in front of Coronel and looked at him earnestly. "Well, in a way, both."

Coronel nodded.

"You want to marry my daughter," Merriwig went on. "Now it is customary, as you know, that to the person to whom I give my daughter, I give also half my kingdom. Naturally, before I make this sacrifice, I wish to be sure that the man to whom—well, of course, you understand."

"That he is worthy of the Princess Hyacinth," said Coronel. "Of course he couldn't be," he added, with a smile.

"*And* worthy of half the kingdom," amended Merriwig. "That he should prove himself this is also, I think, customary."

"Anything that your Majesty suggests—"

"I am sure of it."

He drew up a chair next to Coronel's, and sitting down in it, placed his hands upon his knees and explained the nature of the trial which was awaiting the successful suitor.

"In the ordinary way," he began, "I should arrange something for you with a dragon or whatnot in it. The knowledge that some such ordeal lies before him often enables a suitor to discover, before it is too late, that what he thought was true love is not really the genuine emotion. In your case I feel that an ordeal of this sort is not necessary."

Coronel inclined his head gracefully.

"I do not doubt your valour, and from you, therefore, I ask proof of your cunning. In these days cunning is perhaps the quality of all others demanded of a ruler. We had an excellent example of that," he went on carelessly, "in the war with Barodia that is just over, where the whole conflict was settled by a little idea which—"

"A very wonderful idea, your Majesty."

"Well, well," said Merriwig, looking very

pleased. "It just happened to come off, that's all. But that is what I mean when I say that cunning may be of even more importance than valour. In order to win the hand of my daughter and half my kingdom, it will be necessary for you to show a cunning almost more than human."

He paused, and Coronel did his best in the interval to summon up a look of superhuman guile into his very frank and pleasant countenance.

"You will prove yourself worthy of what you ask me for," said Merriwig solemnly, "by persuading Prince Udo to return to Araby—alone."

Coronel gasped. The thing was so easy that it seemed almost a shame to accept it as the condition of his marriage. To persuade Udo to do what he was only longing to do did not call for superhuman qualities of any kind. For a moment he had an impulse to tell the King so, but he suppressed it. After all, he thought, if the King wants cunning, and if I make a great business of doing something absurdly easy, then he is getting it.

Merriwig, simple man, mistook his emotions.

"I see," he said, "that you are appalled by the difficulty of the ordeal in front of you. You may well be so. You have known his Royal Highness longer than I have, but even in our short acquaintance I have discovered that he takes a hint with extraordinary slowness. To bring it home to him with the right mixture of tact and insistence that Araby needs his immediate presence—alone—may well tax the most serpentine of minds."

"I can but try it," said the serpentine one simply.

The King jumped up and shook him warmly by the hand.

"You think you can do it?" he said excitedly.

"If Prince Udo does not start back to Araby tomorrow—"

"Alone," said Merriwig.

"Alone—then I shall have failed in my task."

"My dear," said the King to his daughter as she kissed him good night that evening, "I believe you are going to marry a very wise young man."

"Of course I am, Father."

"I only hope you'll be as happy with him as I shall be with—as I was with your mother." Though how he's going to bring it off, he added to himself, is more than I can think.

22

The Seventeen Volumes Go Back Again

KING MERRIWIG OF Eastern Euralia sat at breakfast on his castle walls. He lifted the gold cover from the gold dish in front of him, selected a trout, and conveyed it carefully to his gold plate. When you have an aunt . . . But I need not say that again.

King Coronel of Western Euralia sat at breakfast on *his* castle walls. He lifted the gold cover from the gold dish in front of him, selected a trout, and conveyed it carefully to his gold plate. When your wife's father has an aunt . . .

Prince Udo of Araby sat at breakfast . . . But one must draw the line somewhere. I refuse to follow Udo through any more meals. Indeed, I think there has been quite enough eating drinking in this book already. Quite enough of everything in fact; but the time has nearly come to say goodbye.

Let us speed the Prince of Araby first. His departure from Euralia was sudden; five minutes' conversation with Coronel convinced him that there had been a mistake about Belvane's feelings for him, and that he could leave for Araby in perfect safety.

"You must come and see us again," said Merriwig heartily as he shook him by the hand.

"Yes, do," said Hyacinth.

There are two ways of saying this sort of thing, and theirs was the second way. So was Udo's, when he answered that he would be delighted.

It was just a week later that the famous double wedding was celebrated in Euralia. As an occasion for speechmaking by King Merriwig and largesse-throwing by Queen Belvane, it demanded (and got) a whole chapter to itself in Roger's History. I have Roger on my side at last. The virtues he denied to the Countess he cannot but allow to the Queen.

Nor could Hyacinth resist her any longer. Belvane upon her palfrey, laughter in her eyes and roses in her cheeks, her lips slightly parted with eagerness as she flings her silver to the crowd, adorably conscious of her childishness and yet glorying in it, could have no enemies on that day.

"She is a dear," said Hyacinth to Coronel. "She will make a wonderful Queen."

"I know a Queen worth two of her," said Coronel.

"But you do admire her, don't you?"

"Not particularly."

"Oh, Coronel, you must," said Hyacinth, but she felt very happy all the same.

They rode off the next day to their kingdom. The Chancellor had had an exciting week; for seven successive evenings he had been extremely mysterious and reserved to his wife, but now his business was finished and King Merriwig reigned over Eastern Euralia and King Coronel over the West.

Let us just take a look at Belvane's diary before we move on to the last scene.

"*Thursday, September Fifteenth,*" it says. "Became good."

Now for the last scene.

King Merriwig sat in Belvane's garden. They had spent the morning revising their joint book of poetry for publication. The first set of verses was entirely Merriwig's own. It went like this:

"Bo, boll, bill, bole.
Wo, woll, will, wole."

A note by the authors called attention to the fact that it could be begun from either end. The rest of the poems were mainly by Belvane, Merriwig's share in them consisting of a "Capi-

243

tal," or an "I like that," when they were read out to him; but an epic commonly attributed to Charlotte Patacake had crept in somehow.

"A person to see your Majesty," said a flunkey, appearing suddenly.

"What sort of person?" asked Merriwig.

"A sort of person, your Majesty."

"See him here, dear," said Belvane, as she got up. "I have things to do in the Palace."

She left him; and by and by the flunkey returned with the stranger. He was a pleasant-looking person with a round clean-shaven face; something in the agricultural way, to judge from his clothes.

"Well?" said Merriwig.

"I desire to be your Majesty's swineherd," said the other.

"What do you know of swineherding?"

"I have a sort of natural aptitude for it, your Majesty, although I have never actually been one."

"My own case exactly. Now then, let me see—how would you . . ."

The stranger took out a large red handkerchief and wiped his forehead.

"You propose to ask me a few questions, your Majesty?"

"Well, naturally, I—"

"Let me beg of you not to. By all you hold sacred, let me implore you not to confuse me with questions." He drew himself up and thumped his chest with his fist. "I have a feeling for swineherding; it is enough."

Merriwig began to like the man; it was just how he felt about the thing himself.

"I once carried on a long technical conversation with a swineherd," he said reminiscently, "and we found we had much in common. It is an inspiring life."

"It was in just that way," said the stranger, "that I discovered my own natural bent toward it."

"How very odd! Do you know, there's something about your face that I seem to recognize?"

The stranger decided to be frank.

"I owe this face to you," he said simply.

Merriwig looked startled.

"In short," said the other, "I am the late King of Barodia."

Merriwig gripped his hand.

"My dear fellow," he said. "My very dear fellow, of course you are. Dear me, how it brings it all back. And—may I say—what an improvement. Really, I'm delighted to see you. You must tell me all about it. But first some refreshment."

At the word "refreshment" the late King of Barodia broke down altogether, and it was only Merriwig's hummings and hawings and thumpings on the back and (later on) the refreshment itself which kept him from bursting into tears.

"My dear friend," he said, as he wiped his mouth for the last time, "you have saved me."

"But what does it all mean?" asked Merriwig, in bewilderment.

"Listen, and I will tell you."

He told him of the great resolution to which he had come on that famous morning when he awoke to find himself whiskerless. Barodia had no more use for him now as a King, and he on his side was eager to carve out for himself a new life as a swineherd.

"I had a natural gift," he said plaintively, "an instinctive feeling for it. I know I had. Whatever they said about it afterwards—and they said many hard things—I was certain that I had that feeling. I had proved it, you know; there couldn't be any mistake."

"Well?"

"Ah, but they laughed at me. They asked me confusing questions; niggling little questions about the things swine ate and—and things like that. The great general principles of swineherding, the—what I may call the art of herding swine, the whole theory of shepherding pigs in a broad-minded way, all this they ignored. They laughed at me and turned me out with jeers and blows—to starve."

Merriwig patted him sympathetically, and pressed some more food on him.

"I ranged over the whole of Barodia. Nobody

would take me in. It is a terrible thing, my dear Merriwig, to begin to lose faith in yourself. I had to tell myself at last that perhaps there was something about Barodian swine which made them different from those of any other country. As a last hope I came to Euralia; if here, too, I was spurned, then I should know that—"

"Just a moment," said Merriwig, breaking in eagerly. "Who was this swineherd that you talked to—"

"I talked to so many," said the other sadly. "They all scoffed at me."

"No, but the first one; the one that showed you that you had a bent toward it. Didn't you say that—"

"Oh, that one. That was at the beginning of our war. Do you remember telling me that your swineherd had an invisible cloak? It was he that . . ."

Merriwig looked at him sadly, and shook his head.

"My poor friend," he said, "it was me."

They gazed at each other earnestly. Each of them was going over in his mind the exact details of that famous meeting.

"Yes," they murmured together, "it was us."

The King of Barodia's mind raced on through all the bitter months that had followed; he shivered as he thought of the things he had said; the things that had been said to him seemed of small account now.

"Not even a swineherd!" he remarked.

"Come, come," said Merriwig, "look on the bright side; you can always be a King again."

The late King of Barodia shook his head.

"It's a come-down to a man with any pride," he said. "No, I'll stick to my own job. After all, I've been learning these last weeks; at any rate I know that what I do know isn't worth knowing, and that's something."

"Then stay with me," said Merriwig heartily. "My swineherd will teach you your work, and when he retires, you can take it on."

"Do you mean it?"

"Of course I do. I shall be glad to have you about the place. In the evening, when the pigs are asleep, you can come in and have a chat with us."

"Bless you," said the new apprentice; "bless you, your Majesty."

They shook hands on it.

"My dear," said Merriwig to Belvane that evening, "you haven't married a very clever fellow. I discovered this afternoon that I'm not even as clever as I thought I was."

"You don't want cleverness in a King," said Belvane, smiling lovingly at him, "or in a husband."

"What do you want then?"

"Just dearness," said Belvane.

* * *

And now my story is done. With a sigh I unload the seventeen volumes of Euralian History from my desk, carrying them one by one across the library and placing them carefully in the shelf which has been built for them. For some months they have stood, a rampart between me and the world, behind which I have lived in far-off days with Merriwig and Hyacinth and my Lady Belvane. The rampart is gone, and in the bright light of today which streams on to my desk the vision slowly fades. Once on a time . . .

Yet I see one figure clearly still. He is tall and thin, with a white peaked face of which the long inquisitive nose is the outstanding feature. His hair is lank and uncared for; his russet smock, tied in at the waist, wants brushing; his untidy cross-gartered hose shows up the meagreness of his legs. No knightly figure this, yet I look upon him very tenderly. For it is Roger Scurvilegs on his way to the Palace for news.

To Roger too, I must say goodbye. I say it not without remorse, for I feel that I have been hard upon the man to whom I owe so much. Perhaps it will not be altogether goodbye; in his seventeen volumes there are many other tales to be found. Next time (if there be a next time) I owe it to Roger to stand aside and let him tell the story more in his own way. I think he would like that.

But it shall not be a story about Belvane. I saw Belvane (or someone like her) at a country house in Shropshire last summer, and I know that Roger can never do her justice.

THE END

A Note from the Publisher

When this delightful story was first published in 1917, A. A. Milne contributed an Introduction which opened with the words: "The publishers have asked me to introduce this book to you." The present publishers deeply regret that the late Mr. Milne cannot again take on this happy task for a new generation of readers, but still we find (not surprisingly) the author's own words most apt in writing about ONCE ON A TIME.

Mr. Milne wrote: "This is not a children's book. I do not mean by that . . . 'Not for children,' which has an implication all its own. Nor do I mean that children will be unable to appreciate it. . . . But what I do mean is that I wrote it for grown-ups. More particularly for two grown-ups. My wife and myself. . . . This is a Fairy Story; and it is a Fairy Story for grown-ups because I have tried to give some character to the people who wander through its pages. Children prefer incident to character; if character is to be drawn, it must be done broadly, in tar or whitewash. Read the old fairy stories and you will see with what simplicity, with what perfection of method, the child's needs are met. Yet there must have been more in Fairyland than that. . . . Life in Fairyland was not so straightforward as the romancers pretend. The dwellers therein had much our difficulties to meet, much our complex characters wherewith to attack them. Princes were not all good or bad; fairy rings were not always helpful; magic swords and seven-league boots not the only necessary equipment for fighter and traveller. The inhabitants of that blessed country were simpler than we; more credulous; but they were real men and women. I have tried to do justice to them."

In the preface to a later edition published in the early twenties, Mr. Milne was less certain about just who would most enjoy his book. He was certain about one thing, however: of all his books written up to then, he considered *Once on a Time* his "best one." He added: "For whom, then, is the book intended? That is the trouble. Unless I can say, 'For those, young or old, who like the things which I like,' I find it difficult to answer. Is it a children's book? Well, what do we mean by that? Is *The Wind in the Willows* a children's book? Is *Alice in Wonderland*? Is *Treasure Island*? These are masterpieces which we read with pleasure as children, but with how much more pleasure when we are grown-up. In any case, what do we mean by 'children'? A boy of three, a girl of six, a boy of ten, a girl of fourteen—are they all to like the same thing? And is a book 'suitable for a boy of twelve' any more likely to please a boy of twelve than a modern novel is likely to please a man of thirty-seven; even if the novel be described truly as 'suitable for a man of thirty-seven'? I confess that I cannot grapple with these difficult problems. But I am very sure of this: that no one can write a book which children will like, unless he write it for himself first.

". . . But as you can see, I am still finding it difficult to explain just what sort of book it is. Perhaps no explanation is necessary. Read in it what you like; read it to whomever you like; it can only fall into one of the two classes. Either you will enjoy it, or you won't.

"It is that sort of book."

It is, indeed, "that sort of book" but we feel Mr. Milne has seriously underestimated the need for children of all ages to escape into a *believable* Fairyland, two World Wars and nearly fifty years after the rather more innocent days when he lovingly wrote *Once on a Time*.

A Note from the Editor

For most of us childhood evokes a fairy-tale world dimly and pleasurably remembered. But Milne saw the fairylands of childhood for the tough-minded battlegrounds they were, and he chose to adapt that world for adult purposes in his first novel. *Once on a Time* was written during World War I, with France on the horizon for Milne, who described himself as only an Amateur Soldier. This book about, "a Prince and Princess and a Wicked Countess" was dictated during stolen moments as his regiment trained. Before the war ended, Milne would be transferred to the War Office, where his Intelligence task was the preparation of propaganda. It must have been a service that he hated, because Milne was ever after implacably and constantly a foe of war—and untruths.

First and foremost, *Once on a Time* is written in response to all the propaganda about fairyland. "Life in fairyland," he said, "was not so straightfoward as the romancers pretend. The dwellers therein had much our difficulties to meet, much our complex characters wherewith to attack them. Princes were not all good or bad; fairy rings were not always helpful; magic swords and seven-league boots not the only necessary equipment for fighter and traveller. The inhabitants of that blessed country were simpler than we; more credulous; but they were real men and women. I have tried to do justice to them." Justice seems not to me to be Milne's main accomplishment here, but as a corrective and as a delightful story *Once on a Time* can hardly be equalled. It was, as he said, "not a children's book. I do not mean that children will be unable to appreciate it. . . . But what I do mean is that I wrote it for grown-ups."